Bauble, Me and the Family Tree

Bauble, Me and the Family Tree
An original concept by author Jenny Moore
© Jenny Moore

Cover artwork by Kiersten Eagan

Published by MAVERICK ARTS PUBLISHING LTD
Studio 11, City Business Centre, 6 Brighton Road,
Horsham, West Sussex, RH13 5BB
+44 (0) 1403 256941
© Maverick Arts Publishing Limited September 2020

A CIP catalogue record for this book is available
at the British Library.

ISBN: 978-1-84886-678-2

Bauble, Me and the Family Tree

JENNY MOORE

For Dafydd, Lucy and Daniel, with love

"I saw Mommy kissing Santa Claus,
Underneath the mistletoe last night."
- The Ronettes

1

UNDERNEATH
THE WISHING BOW

Here's the thing: when Bauble tells you a fact, there's a 99.999999 percent chance it's true. I know she was only seven when this all started, but my brainbox of a sister has always been teeth-grindingly clever for her age. For *anyone's* age. On a super-swot-chops scale of one to ten, she'd be a fourteen and a half, easy. Actually, she'd probably break the scale with the sheer power of her Bauble Brains, which is why you should never ever agree to play Trivial Pursuit with her. Not even the Sports Edition. She knows everything under the sun and everything over it too. Only this time she was wrong. My genius of a little sister was one hundred percent wrong. Even *I* could see that.

"I saw Mummy kissing Father Christmas," she whispered, through a mouthful of mushy Dino Rocks.

Or it could have been Honey Raisin Boulders now that I think about it. There was something suspiciously dark and dried-fruitish lurking between her front teeth. "Underneath the wishing bow," she added, balancing her spoon on the tip of her left index finger. Her right finger was scrolling down a website called 'Everything You Always Wanted to Know About Fulcrums and Pivot Points'. She always reads sciencey stuff like that at breakfast, which is why she's allowed on her tablet and I'm not. For some reason, checking the latest football scores doesn't count as an educational activity.

"You mean 'Santa Claus'," I said, pleased to be correcting *her* for once. I guessed she was talking about that cheesy Christmas song—you know the one I mean. "And it's 'underneath the mistletoe'. Not 'wishing bow'."

"No it wasn't." Bauble shook her head and the spoon fell back onto the table with a clatter. "Why would anyone be kissing under mistletoe in *August?* It was definitely a wishing bow." She pointed towards the kitchen door. "That new red one there."

Ah. *That* one. Our house is full of wishing bows. I used to think that was normal—that *everyone* had old

present bows dangling down over their doorways—
but it turned out it's just us. Dad died the day before
Mum's birthday, you see, back when I was two and
Bauble was still in Mum's tummy. Only no one found
the posh chocolates he'd hidden at the bottom of the
wardrobe for another whole year, and Mum had to
throw them away. But she tucked the wrapping paper
under her pillow and hung the pink bow up in the
bedroom doorway so it trailed down like an exotic
flower.

In fact, that's one of my first ever memories: Mum
standing underneath the bow with my new baby sister
cuddled into her chest, sobbing. I expect Bauble was
crying too—she did a *lot* of that when she was little—
but it's Mum I remember: "I wish you could have seen
her," she kept saying, as if Dad was there in the room
with us, listening in. "I wish you could have held her.
Just once." Her face was red and blotchy, all twisted
up in the wrong places, with tears and snot dripping
off the end of her chin. It was horrible. Not the sort of
memory you want at all. But that's when it began.
That's when *I* started wishing under the bow too—
sometimes for a chocolate biscuit, but usually just for
Mum to stop crying. And then, after my next birthday,

I got a bow all of my own: a blue and green paper ribbon one, in pride of place over my bedroom door. There's a long row of them now, reaching right across the doorway, which is just as well as we get through a lot of wishes in our house.

Bauble pushed away her unfinished breakfast and stood up. Her eyes had gone all big and shiny-looking, as if she'd spotted a bookshop or a library. At first I thought she'd had an idea for a new pivot point experiment, but that wasn't it at all. No, she was simply checking the coast was clear before she carried on with her story. Luckily Mum was still upstairs, sorting out piles of dirty washing.

"She was standing right here," Bauble whispered, tapping the floor with her toe to mark the spot. "And Father Christmas was here, with his back to the stairs. And then he leaned in really close and put his arms round her…" She stretched out her hands, puckering up her lips like a constipated goldfish. It was like one of those crime reconstructions on *Junior Police Force*, only more gruesome. I'd rather watch a made-up robbery than kissing any day. "And that's when they started kissin—"

"Stop it. That's enough." *More* than enough. I shut

my eyes and put my hands over my ears before she added any sound effects, trying to delete the image from my brain. Easier said than done. Once I'd pictured it I couldn't *un*picture it again. Yuck!

"So what do you think?" she said at last, coming back to the table to carry on with her cutlery experiments. "Should we say something, or wait for her to tell us herself?" Bauble rebalanced her spoon on her finger, only the other way up this time. I could see the insides of her nostrils reflected in the metal.

"Hmm," I said, pretending to weigh up all the options. "I think the best thing to do would be to forget all about it." *And* never *mention it again.* She'd clearly imagined the whole thing but that didn't mean *I* had to imagine it too. I picked up my own spoon, breathed on it a few times, and stuck it to the end of my nose. With Mum out of the way, it was the perfect chance to beat my one minute and thirty-seven second spoon-balancing record. Without getting told off for playing with cutlery, I mean. When my little sister does things like that, it's called 'science'. When *I* do, it's called 'messing around'.

Bauble wasn't giving up so easily though. "Perhaps she's been waiting to tell us all this time, only she can't find the right words..." She paused, rubbing at her teeth with her other finger as if she was trying to work out a particularly tricky problem. Or dislodge a stray bit of raisin. "But what if he made her swear on Granny's life not to let anyone know about their secret time together? Not even us. And she can't break her promise in case Granny gets struck by lightning?"

"Huh? What do you mean?" She'd completely lost me now. One: we don't even *have* a granny. We don't have an anybody, except for Mum, the Uncle Mikes, and each other. Two: Mum has never had any trouble finding words. Seriously, she'll talk to *anyone* about *anything*. I once found her in the garden chatting to a woodlouse. And three: well, three, I didn't have a clue what she was on about. Last time I checked, we were talking about snogging Santas and Christmas songs.

"What I *mean*," said Bauble, "is should we tell her we know who he is—ask if we can see him too—or carry on keeping it a secret?"

Huh? I thought again, only I kept it in my head this time. Who *who* was? Life with an over-intelligent seven-year-old could be really hard work sometimes.

"Twenty-five… twenty-six… twenty-seven," I said instead, counting the seconds out loud to show I had more important things to think about than mystery kissers or imaginary grandmothers. Like a new world record for balancing cutlery on my nose.

"*Please*, Noel," she begged. "It's important we get it right. This is our dad we're talking about."

"HUH?" I turned round so fast the spoon flew all the way across the kitchen and landed in Rudy's cat litter tray. "Our *dad?*"

Bauble nodded. She was all smiles now. "I always knew he was still alive. I just knew it."

2

WHAT'S NEW, PUSSYCAT?

So here's the other thing: my little sister is every bit as stubborn as she is clever. No matter how many times I told her she must have got it wrong—that there was no way our dead dad was actually Father Christmas, flown in on the Rudolph Express for a sneaky summer snog in our kitchen—she stuck to her story like chewing gum on the bottom of a shoe.

"How do you explain *this* then?" she said, pouncing on a stray bit of tinsel that was worming its way underneath the oven.

"Easy," I lied. "That'll be from the… you know, the erm…" What *was* it doing there? We didn't even *have* any tinsel, as far as I knew. Mum and I always make paper chains for the tree instead, out of her old photography magazines. Bauble helps too, in theory, but she gets distracted by the sight of all those words and ends up reading boring old articles about lenses and light levels.

She dangled the tinsel in front of my nose, making it dance like a snake. Like one of those charmed snakes in cartoons that come twisting out of their clay jar when someone plays the magic tune. Not an actual disco-dancing viper, though that *would* have been cool. This particular strand of dancing tinsel was silver, with shiny red bits running all the way down the middle, and I didn't have the foggiest idea what it was doing hiding under our cooker.

"Okay, so I can't actually explain *that*," I admitted, "but that doesn't prove anything." I gave her my best 'caring big brother' smile—like a normal smile only without any teeth showing—and took the tinsel out of her hand. "I'm sorry, Bauble, but Dad's never coming back. Not now, and not down our chimney at Christmas either. It doesn't matter how hard we wish…"

I *definitely* knew what I was talking about now. I'd wished on every single wishing bow in the house over the years—screwing up my eyes and wishing until it hurt—but Dad was still just as dead as he always had been. No. Wishing wasn't going to bring him back any more than crying.

"But we've got each other," I told her, "and Mum and Uncle Mike. And the other Uncle Mike…"

I'm not sure Bauble was listening. "What about our birthdays then?" she said.

Oh dear. Time for another caring big brother smile, with added head-shaking for good measure.

"No," I said, stretching the words out long and slow to try and make them less painful. "I'm afraid he won't be coming back for our birthdays either. That doesn't mean he won't be thinking of us though, watching over us…" To be honest, I couldn't really picture Dad as an angel—in fact I couldn't really picture him at all after all these years—but it was kind of nice to think there was someone up there in the clouds, keeping an eye on us. Like a fluffy white superhero.

"*No*," said Bauble, almost fizzing with frustration. "I mean, the *dates* of our birthdays. Think about it."

So I did. I thought about my birthday being on the 25th of September—less than one month to go!—and Bauble's being the day after that. Between you and me, it's a bit of a rubbish arrangement really, because we often end up sharing birthday parties and cakes. Sometimes even presents.

"Both our birthdays are nine months after Christmas," said Bauble. "Nine months after Father Christmas finishes his deliveries and sneaks off to visit his secret wife." She looked very pleased with herself all of a sudden. "And how long do pregnancies last?"

"Nine months," I agreed. "But still…" Maybe she'd dreamt it all. That was the only logical explanation I could think of.

"And then there are our names," she went on. "Everyone knows Noël is French for Christmas."

Really? That would be everyone except me then. Miss Portlyhead never mentioned *that* when she was teaching us how to count up to ten in French and order a *pain au chocolat*. Unless that was when I was off with chickenpox last December. *I'd* always assumed Mum named me after that beardy chap on the telly who does the afternoon game shows. She's got a bit of a soft spot for men with facial hair.

There was a loud thump above our heads and we both jumped as if we'd been caught doing something we shouldn't. *Talking* about something we shouldn't. I waited a moment, listening out for footsteps on the stairs, but it seemed quiet enough.

"I guess Noel *might* be a Christmassy name then," I agreed, dropping my voice down to a whisper. To be honest, my money was still on the beardy gameshow man with the terrible jumpers. "But you're not *really* Bauble, so that doesn't count."

It was my fault (surprise, surprise) that she ended up with such a stupid nickname. It's no good asking a three-year-old what they think of a round, shiny-faced baby and expecting a sensible answer though, is it? Who knows, maybe I really *did* think she looked like a Christmas decoration. Or maybe I was trying to say 'bubble', seeing as the Uncle Mikes had just given me a giant bottle of bubble mixture as a 'new big brother' present. Either way, Bauble's what everyone thought I said and, worse luck for her, that's the name that stuck.

"I mean 'Holly'," she hissed, putting her hands on her hips for added emphasis. "You know, that spiky green stuff with the red berries that everyone puts on their *Christmas* cards."

This wasn't getting us anywhere.

"I *saw* her," Bauble insisted. "I saw Mummy…" She froze as a rolled-up pair of pants came bowling in through the doorway.

"Saw me doing what?" asked Mum, staggering in after the pants, her face hidden behind a tangled heap of dirty socks and t-shirts.

"Er… picking snotty tissues up from under Noel's bed," said Bauble, quick as anything. She shot me a meaningful look. I wasn't quite sure *what* it meant exactly, but I did my best to play along. Maybe—just maybe—she really *had* seen something strange going on in the kitchen the night before. And maybe it was my job as her big brother to help her get to the bottom of it all, before she got too excited about Dad sweeping us off in his sleigh. But blurting out clumsy questions at the breakfast table wasn't the way to go about it. *So Mum, what's this I hear about a new beardy boyfriend? What football team does he support? Will he be moving in with us? Are you going to get married?* No. Sneaky investigations on the quiet, that was more like it. That way no one got hurt. Not Mum—not after everything she'd been through—and hopefully not Bauble either.

"Oh, yeah," I muttered. "Sorry about that. Had a bit of a runny nose last night." It's not like I *mean* to drop tissues all round the bedroom. They must crawl off my bedside table when I'm not looking.

"Twelve tissues, seven football magazines and two apple cores," agreed Mum, who'd obviously been keeping count. "Not to mention that bag of dirty football kit balanced on top of your wardrobe. At least it *was*…"

Ah, yes. That would probably explain the loud thump.

"I think a quick tidy up might be in order once you've finished breakfast," she said, sounding surprisingly cheerful for someone who'd spent the last five minutes with their head in a basket of dirty washing, dodging flying football boots. "Don't you? And while you're at it, perhaps you'd like to retrieve that spoon from Rudy's litter tray," she added, breaking into a grin. Yes, a grin, and a big grin at that.

Strange, I thought. *Very strange*. Don't get me wrong, it wasn't the grin itself that was odd—Mum's a pretty smiley sort of person in general. But not when it comes to finding cutlery in with the cat poo. I'd never seen her smile at *that* before. And things were about to get even stranger. That's right, I'm talking singing. I'm talking dancing round the kitchen, singing away at the top of her voice:

"What's new pussycat? Whoa-oa-oa-oa-ah."

Mum never sings. I mean never. And if you've ever heard her tuneless caterwauling, you'll know why.

3

I'LL BE HOLMES FOR CHRISTMAS

For the record, I still thought Bauble was barking up the wrong Christmas tree. But seeing Mum in such high spirits only made me more determined to keep quiet until we knew more. That's my excuse, anyway, for what happened next...

"So," said Bauble, when Mum went out into the garden with the clothes she'd just taken out of the machine, still singing away to herself. She was on laundry overdrive that day. "Shall we ask her or not?"

A simple 'no' would have been fine. A nice straightforward 'Better not. Let's wait and see if we can find out any more about him first.' Like if he even existed outside of Bauble's imagination. But for some reason I didn't go for the simple option. I guess I thought if we made it into a game—turned the whole thing into a bit of fun—then she wouldn't be too crushed when she realised the truth: Dad wasn't Father Christmas. Or the Easter Bunny. And definitely not the Tooth Fairy. He was just dead.

So I picked up my spoon again—watch out, here comes the really cringey, embarrassing bit—and stuck it in my mouth like an old-fashioned pipe. Actually it must have been Bauble's spoon now I come to think about it, because mine was still nestling in the steaming cat litter. That would have been gross. Anyway, I took a few sucks on my pipe spoon, nodded wisely, and said (in my very best Sherlock Holmes voice), "Smellementary, my dear Snotson. We say nothing until we've examined all the evidence and completed our investigations."

Bauble giggled. She might have the brains of a boring grown-up but her sense of humour's just as childish as mine. Anything to do with snot passes for comic genius as far as she's concerned. Lucky for us, I'm *full* of snot jokes. Full of snot, too, most of the time. Just ask my dirty tissue collection.

"Will there be any baying black hounds?" she asked.

Cue a blank look from me.

"You know," she said, "like in 'The Hound of the Baskervilles'?"

Make that two blank looks. Between you and me, I'd never actually read any Sherlock Holmes stories. Never even seen a Sherlock Holmes film. My sole knowledge of the great detective came from that two-minute trailer they kept showing on telly. The one with the pipe-smoking and the whole 'Elementary, my dear Watson' speech.

"What about Holmes' violin?" asked Bauble. "I know! I could play the recorder!"

"That won't be necessary," I said, quickly. "Who needs hounds and violins when you've got… erm… when you've got… notebooks. Yes! That's it. Proper detectifying notebooks. That's what we need. Meet me in the downstairs toilet at oh-nine-hundred hours, and all will be revealed."

I checked my watch: 8.54 a.m.! Time really does fly when you're having is-my-father-Father-Christmas fun. "On second thoughts, better make that ten o'clock instead."

It turns out I'm not the world's greatest notebook

maker. I got glue stuck to my fingers, ear wax stuck in the glue (don't ask), and a nasty scissor cut in my favourite Mutant Monkey Man pyjamas. In the end, I gave up altogether and went to look for some exercise books in Mum's study. She keeps all our old school stuff in there. And that's when I saw it. A red hat, hanging off the back of her new spinny-round chair. A floppy red hat with white fur along the bottom and a big white pom-pom stuck on top. Yes. That's right. A Santa hat!

My breath stuck in my throat. Or maybe I just forgot to breathe in all the excitement because, for a moment or two there, I actually believed it. Crazy, I know. But all that talk of Mum kissing under the wishing bow… and then the hat waiting there for me like a big fat clue… What if Bauble was right? What if Dad wasn't dead, after all? Just dead famous? It could be like that bit in *Star Wars* when Darth Vader tells Luke who he really is: "I am your father (Christmas)". Only with less heavy breathing and a bit more ho-ho-ho-ing.

Then the sensible bit of my brain cut in and ruined everything. There was nothing magic or North Pole-y about *this* hat. Not when I looked at it properly. No. It was just a cheap old dressing-up one, like the Uncle Mikes wear when we go round to theirs for Christmas dinner. The daydream disappeared again, and Dad went back to being dead. Thanks a bunch, brain.

I carried on hunting for old exercise books, trying to tell myself I didn't care. That I didn't need a dad anyway. I even sang the start of 'I saw Mommy Kissing Santa Claus' in my best squeaky chipmunk voice, to prove what a big joke it all was. Ha ha ha! I got as far as 'underneath the mistletoe last night,' and then realised I didn't know any more words after that. Probably just as well really, because I was getting horrible kissy pictures in my head again—not what you want when you've just had your breakfast. So I swapped over to the Mutant Monkey Man theme tune instead:

Watch out, here he comes, swinging through the city!
Bad Cat better scram, or "Sweet Banana Jam",
He'll be squealing like an itty-bitty kitty…

But wait a minute. What was that? No. Not a hat this time. It was a black metal box file, hidden away behind a stash of old photography magazines. With a little handwritten label on the front that said 'Family Documents'. As far as I knew, we kept all that sort of stuff—school reports, bank statements and any other important letters—in the broken bureau in the sitting room.

Hmm, I thought, feeling surprisingly like a proper detective. If I still had Bauble's spoon I might have sneaked another Sherlock Holmes puff on it, just in case. I mean, just in case it gave me any ideas. Because I was pretty sure I'd never seen a mysterious black box lurking round the place before. As for what was inside… Well, I didn't have a clue. Not a sausage. Secret Santa photographs? Ancient treasure maps? False spy passports? It could be anything really.

And there was only one way to find out.

4

SHERLOCK HOLMELESS

Holey Penguin Pants! It was locked! And no matter how hard I rattled the rusty gold clips and jiggled the corner of a ruler inside the keyhole, it stayed locked. Which was a bit odd really. On second thoughts, make that a *lot* odd, because Mum's not exactly known for her brilliant security. She once left the front door open for a whole day when we went to the seaside—it's a miracle the telly was still there when we got back. And she's always putting things down to take a photo, then panicking when she can't find them again afterwards. So what was she doing with a locked box file? A hidden one at that?

If I'd been curious to see what was inside before, suddenly I was *desperate*. What could be so secret it needed hiding away under lock and key? Was it something to do with Dad? And who was Mum hiding it away *from* exactly? Because the only other people who ever went in her study were Bauble and me, and we didn't count because we *were* family. Technically speaking, anything marked 'family documents' belonged to us too. At least that's what I told myself as I started hunting through her desk for the missing key.

It wasn't easy. The top drawer was so full of stuff it made my bedroom look like the cover of *Posh House Magazine*. You know, the one they always have in the dentist's waiting room, that's been there since January 2003. There were broken pencils and tangled-up rubber bands, old receipts and empty sweet wrappers, five coupons for a shop that closed down the year before, and a horrible shrivelled-looking thing that might once have been a peach. That was my guess anyway. Either a dried out peach or a dried out giraffe poo. But that was nothing compared to what I found in the middle drawer...

A photograph. Okay. That's not so surprising given that Mum's a photographer. But it was the person *in* the photograph that made me gasp out loud. It was Mrs Manzo, who works in the butcher's shop, as I'd never seen her before. To be honest, I never wanted to see her like that again either. I mean, who wants to eat lamb chops from a woman in a bright pink bikini, with a giant pork pie balanced on her head? Seriously. A pork pie. Like it was a hat or something. Oh yes, and don't forget the necklace of raw sausages strung around her neck. Gross! I put it back where I found it and tried to wipe the image from my brain.

I went more carefully after that, in case I stumbled across something even worse. Like a picture of *Mr* Manzo in a pair of skimpy swimming trunks, with giant beef burgers stuck to his bum cheeks. Double gross! But there could have been a whole army of meaty butchers' buttocks waiting in the next drawer down and I'd never have found them. Because just as I lifted up an old newspaper cutting from the top of the pile, the door swung open and Mum came in.

"Oh!" she cried when she saw me, jumping like Rudy when someone treads on his tail. "You gave me a fright! What are you doing in here?"

"Nothing." I shoved the drawer back in with my knee and sprang to my feet, stuffing the newspaper cutting down the back of my pyjamas. And then I realised how guilty that 'nothing' made me sound, so

I tried again. "I was just looking for… erm…" *Think, brain, think!* I guess I should have stuck to the truth— *I was just looking for some old exercise books*—but I panicked. What with the Santa hat and the mysterious black box—not to mention Mrs Manzo's saucy sausage snap—I couldn't quite remember what I'd gone in there for. "…For a pen," I blurted out. My cheeks felt like I'd been out in the sun too long. "That's it. I was just looking for a pen."

Mum smiled back at me. It was a bit of a suspicious-looking one, but it *was* a smile.

"What's wrong with the pens in the pen pot?" she asked.

Oops. "Oh yes. There they are! Silly me."

Okay, so looking for a pen was a stupid cover story. There must have been fifteen or more poking out the top of the yucky brown Mother's Day mug I made in Year 4. Only it stopped being a mug when the handle fell off and turned into a pen pot instead. And there it was, slap bang in front of my nose, with pens spilling out the top and a homemade postcard propped against the side where the handle used to be. Someone had drawn a cartoon robin in a Santa hat on the front of the card, with a little pencilled message underneath: *My*

Christmas came early this year! F x

Mum made a sudden lunge for the robin picture, pushing it under a pile of bills as if she didn't want me to see it. But I wasn't interested in cartoon birds and pencilled kisses—not at that exact moment, anyway—I was too busy shuffling back from the desk, making the most of the distraction. Complete with some fake-coughing to cover up the crackling newspaper sound coming from my bottom. Besides, I had other things to think about.

Ask her about the black box, said a little voice in my head. *What's the worst that can happen?*

I was tempted. I really was. But I couldn't think of a way to say it that didn't sound like I'd been going through her stuff. Probably because I *had* been going through her stuff. I still had the crackly bottom to prove it. What if she got cross? Suddenly that 'Family Documents' label seemed rather less important than the fact it was locked.

I glanced back at the box, trying to make up my mind. Say something? Or grab hold of a pen and get out of there? And then Mum made up my mind for me. She must have followed my gaze—turning her head round to see what I was looking at—and the smile slipped right off the bottom of her face.

"What's that doing out?" Her hands were already on her hips and her voice had gone all sharp and jaggedy. Not like her usual voice at all.

"Nothing," I said. Again. It was an even worse answer second time around.

"Nothing? Don't you 'nothing' me, Noel. I'm serious."

Uh-oh. I felt sick in my stomach all of a sudden. Really sick. What had I done?

"You keep your nose out of that box," Mum hissed. She was pale-faced and furious-looking now, the muscle in the side of her neck pulsing like crazy. In and out it went. In and out, as if there was something inside trying to bounce right through her skin. I don't think I'd ever seen her so mad. "It's private. You shouldn't even be in here."

What? Since when?

"Sorry. I'm really sorry," I stammered, feeling guilty and cross all at the same time. Guilty because I hadn't meant to upset her. Because I knew I shouldn't have been nosing through her desk in the first place. And cross with myself for getting caught. "I didn't open it," I added, as if it was a matter of choice, rather than not being able to find the key. "I don't know what's inside."

"You didn't see anything at all?" The pulsing in her neck seemed to slow down a bit, a touch of colour creeping back into her cheeks.

"No. Nothing." Apart from the robin postcard from 'F' (whoever he or she was) and the photo of Mrs Manzo, of course, which I'd give anything to un-see. "Cross my heart."

"Just as well," she said, quickly. "Make sure you keep it that way. It's got nothing to do with you. Do you understand?"

I nodded, not knowing what else to say to make things right. At that precise moment in time, I couldn't have cared less what was in the stupid box. I just wanted Mum to stop being all weird and angry with me. To go back to normal. I kept on nodding.

She took a few deep breaths, clutching onto the bookcase as if she was trying not to fall over.

"Right. Then I suggest you go and sort out under your bed like I asked you to," she said at last, her voice softening. Still cross, but normal cross. "And you'd better get dressed while you're up there as well. We've got to be at the optician's for quarter past ten."

"The optician's?" That was the first I'd heard about it. "Can't Bauble and I stay behind with Uncle Mike instead?" What I really meant was, *Why don't we keep out of your way and give you a chance to calm down?* I didn't dare say it out loud though. "I promised her we'd do some..." Some what, exactly? Detecting? Snooping about? I wasn't sure that was a good thing to admit to under the circumstances. "...something nice together."

"And how exactly is the optician supposed to check your eyes if you're both next door with Uncle Mike?"

Oh. So the appointment was for us. Fifteen minutes of staring at letters that didn't actually spell anything, and having lights shone in our eyes. Great.

"I don't know why you're acting so surprised," said Mum. "I told you I booked you both in when I got my glasses tightened last week."

No, I thought. *You didn't. You told us you'd found a piano teacher called Mr Marsh, but you didn't say anything about eye tests.* Still, she wasn't shouting anymore, that was the main thing. And her neck had stopped pulsing altogether. Normal Mum was back. At least I thought she was, until she flung her arms round me and started crying.

"Oh Noel," she sobbed. "I'm so sorry."

Woah! Where did that *come from?*

"Don't worry," I mumbled. "It's fine." Talking was a bit tricky with my mouth pressed into her armpit, but I did my best. "Bauble and I can always do our thing later. And I guess we *are* due an eye check."

Then, just as suddenly, she was laughing. As far as I could tell, anyway. It was hard to be sure with her t-shirt pressed tight over my ear and tears still dripping down into my hair. "Oh Noel," she said again. "I didn't mean to snap at you like that, sweetheart. It's just… well… it's my job to protect you. You understand that, don't you?"

"Yes," I mumbled into her armpit, clenching my bum cheeks as the newspaper cutting started slipping down my trousers. Not that I understood *any* of it. I didn't have the first clue what had just happened, or what all the crazy tears and hugging were in aid of. I didn't know who the 'F' on the postcard was, and I *still* didn't know what was in the mysterious black box. Some Sherlock Holmes I was turning out to be.

5

A BULB A DAY KEEPS THE VAMPIRES AWAY

Bauble clearly didn't know who 'F' was, though she claimed it was short for Father (as in Father Christmas). And she didn't know who the man in the newspaper cutting was either—some beardy bloke in Chapworth called Mr Coffee Stain Okenson, who'd won an award for his 'Vampires & Zombies' computer game. Coffee Stain wasn't his real name of course but it might as well have been, thanks to the big brown mark over half the cutting. Goodness only knew what he was doing in Mum's desk because she hates computer games. At least, she hates *me* playing them when I'm supposed to be doing homework or tidying my room. Perhaps she was a secret vampire slayer, or a stealth zombie zapper, waiting until we were safely tucked up in bed before heading into battle against the undead. I couldn't quite see it though.

The optician's appointment had come as a surprise to Bauble as well, which meant Mum *definitely* forgot to tell us.

"She must have had other things on her mind lately," Bauble whispered, as we squished onto the waiting area sofa beside a round, wheezy man with super-strong garlic breath. Seriously, he could have seen off a vampire attack from ten miles away, just by blowing. "Like Daddy's visit," she added. "And that's why she got all cross and weepy with you today— because he's gone home to the North Pole and she misses him. Because all she's got left is an empty hat and a picture of a robin."

"You didn't *see* her," I whispered back, choosing to ignore that last bit. Perhaps I shouldn't have said anything about the Santa 'clues' I'd found. Perhaps it was wrong to keep encouraging Bauble's crazy idea. "She wasn't just cross, she was..." What exactly? It was like there was something dangerous inside that box she was trying to protect me from. Like when a wild animal thinks someone's threatening their young. But what could be bad enough to turn Mum into a snarling tiger? Did I even want to find out?

She was back to her old self now, which was the main thing. There she was, still chattering away to the receptionist, oblivious to the massive queue building up behind her. "And Mary from the butcher's, of course," she was saying. "As you've never seen her before!"

I pricked up my ears. That must be Mrs Manzo she was talking about. Skimpy bikini-wearing, sausage-necklaced Mrs Manzo. Bleurgh!

The receptionist let out a funny snorting noise, as if a laugh had gone down her nose by mistake. "I can't wait to get my hands on it," she grinned. "It'll have pride of place on my kitchen wall."

Hang on a minute. Did I hear that right? The photograph was for *her?* Why would she want sausagey Mrs Manzo staring down at her while she was cooking? While she was drinking her tea every morning? Why would *anyone* want that? Apart from Mr Manzo maybe…

"And just wait until you see Mr March," said Mum. "You're in for a treat there!"

Holey Santa Socks! Did that mean Mum was snapping strange sausage pictures of other people too? Yuck, yuck, and more yuck. I mean, I knew she sometimes talked about branching out into other photography work when the wedding season came to an end. But I didn't think she meant *meat modelling*.

"You'll have to remind me," said the receptionist. "Who's Mr March?"

I leaned sideways in my seat, risking another garlicky noseful from Puffy the Vampire Slayer, so I could hear better. *I* wanted to know who this Mr March was too, because I'd just had a horrible idea. What if it turned out to be the new piano teacher Mum had found for us? I *thought* she'd said his name was Mr *Marsh*, as in a wet, boggy field. But what if I'd got it wrong? What if it was *March*, as in soldiers in silly hats going *left, right, left?* What if he turned out to be some half-dressed weirdo who balanced pork chops on his head while we were playing tunes?

I didn't get the chance to find out though, because the optician came to fetch us before Mum could answer.

"Noel and Holly Patermoor?" she said, squinting round the waiting area through the thickest pair of glasses I've ever seen.

Mum sprang into action. "Yes! That's us. Come on kids, up you get."

Puffy the Vampire Slayer let out a massive sigh—I guess he must have thought *he* was next—and we leapt off the sofa as if our bums were on fire. Though in reality it was only our noses.

"Lovely to see you again," Mum called back to the receptionist. "Gosh, look at that enormous queue. Good job we got here when we did."

Oh yes, I thought. *Mum was definitely back to normal.*

I was first into the big black chair, doing my best impression of Mutant Monkey Man trying to escape from The Seat of Doom while the optician adjusted the height: "Help! It's got me! No! Not the Bottom Slicer Cushion of Catastrophe!" Actually I never quite made it to the catastrophe bit, because that's when Mum nudged me in the leg and told me to behave myself. Which I did, of course. After the events of that morning I didn't want to risk getting on the wrong side of her again.

I was the model eye patient after that and got all the way down to the last line of letters on the optician's chart without any problems. I still think it would be more fun if they actually spelt something though, like:

I

D O

N O T

L I K E

P O N G Y

G A R L I C

B R E A T H

Or:

F

I S

N O T

S A N T A

C L A U S

R E A L L Y

Bauble wasn't so lucky with her eye test. She kept saying O when it was quite clearly a C and getting all her Bs and Rs and Es in a muddle. I swear she was making it up completely by the end. It sounds a bit horrible—okay, a lot horrible—but I was secretly pleased. At last, I thought, something I could do better than my little sister! Something other than snot jokes, I mean. But then I felt bad when she finally finished all the different tests and the optician told her she needed glasses.

"Not all the time," she said, eyes bulging at Bauble behind her thick lenses. "Just for long distance stuff like reading things off the whiteboard. We wouldn't want you falling behind with your schoolwork now, would we?"

Ha ha! That was a good one. Bauble could spend the next three years in a blindfold and she'd still be miles ahead of everyone else. In fact, Bauble could spend the next three years at the bottom of a hole and still come out top of the class.

Mum was trying not to laugh too. I could see a mischievous smile dancing round the corners of her mouth but she shook it away again. "Glasses, eh? That's exciting," she said, as if she was trying to convince Bauble it was a good thing.

Hmm. That wasn't *quite* the word I'd have used. Not that there's anything wrong with wearing glasses, obviously, but that doesn't make them *exciting*. Unless they're X-Ray specs, like Mutant Monkey Man's, which let you see through solid walls. That'd be good. If I had a pair of those I'd have been able to see what was inside the black box whether it was locked or not.

It turned out Bauble didn't need any convincing anyway. In fact, she couldn't have looked more pleased.

"Is short-sightedness hereditary?" she asked the optician. "Does it run in families?"

Ah. Cunning! Mum only wore *her* glasses for close reading, which meant she must be long-sighted instead. *Top detecting there, Snotson*, I thought to myself. Though I wasn't sure how it helped Bauble's theory, exactly. I mean, Father Christmas's distance vision must be pretty good when it comes to precision rooftop landings.

"Sometimes," said the optician. "But not always."

Bauble's next set of questions had nothing to do with our investigations:

"Do you have any frames like Gandhi's?" she asked. "Or John Lennon's?"

Who?

Bauble thought for a moment. "Or Velma from *Scooby Doo*?"

That was more like it.

The optician looked baffled. Bauble often has that effect on people.

"Erm... Do you know, I'm not sure. We've got some nice pink flowery ones in at the moment, and a new Disney Princess range..." Her voice trailed away to nothing under the cutting ice of Bauble's glare. "Perhaps you'd like to have a look for yourself," she said, "and I'll get one of our dispensing staff to come and talk you through the different options. Unless you have any more questions...?"

If there really was such a thing as X-ray glasses, would you be able to see everyone's bones? Or would you just be able to see their underwear? That's what I wanted to know. If it turned out to be the underwear option I'd *definitely* take them off before I went in the butcher's shop in future. Before I went anywhere at all, come to that. But I wasn't sure the optician was going to be much help on that score. Besides, Mum was wearing her serious face again, so it probably wasn't the best time to ask. As for the other questions still jumping around in my brain—*What's in the box?* and *Who's Mr Zombie-Zapper Coffee Stain Okenson?*—they'd just have to wait.

6

LIKE FATHER LIKE DAUGHTER

Bauble didn't actually get her glasses for another few days, because they had to send away for the right lenses. She spent most of that time with her head buried in books about eyes and eyesight, leaving me to carry on our investigation on my own. Not that I was following up her Father Christmas theory very hard, it has to be said. Most of my detecting consisted of staring into Mr Okenson's black and white newsprint face, trying to work out what he was doing in Mum's desk drawer.

There was something oddly familiar about him that I couldn't quite put my finger on. Almost like I'd seen him somewhere before, which was pretty unlikely given I'd never been to Chapworth in my life. I didn't even know where it was—I had to ask Bauble. I got this funny feeling when I looked into his eyes though, as if he was trying to tell me something. What was it? There was no date on the section Mum had cut out, but judging by the yellowing paper and faded letters it must've been a few years old. So why had she kept a story about a games designer all that time? Why had she saved it in the first place?

I'd been brooding over the mystery contents of the black box too. I couldn't shake the idea that it was something important to do with Dad. That whatever was inside might somehow bring him back to me. I don't know how exactly, it's hard to explain. Just a feeling, the same as with the newspaper cutting. Every day I headed down to Mum's study to have another look for the missing key. But every day I bottled it again, before I even reached the study door. It was like a never-ending argument pinging backwards and forwards inside my head:

I can't do it.

I've got to do it.

No, it's too risky…

I'm not sure what I was more scared of—getting caught, or not getting caught. Maybe I wouldn't *want* to know what was in there, once I'd actually seen it.

What was Mum trying to protect me from? The fact that Dad was really a vampire? That he'd been killed by zombies? Or did that mean he'd be a zombie too now?

The longer I kept all my crazy ideas bottled up in my head, the more bonkers they became. But it's not like I could talk to anyone else about them. The last thing I wanted to do was upset Mum again. Or Bauble. Besides, Little Miss Super Brains was too busy becoming the world's leading expert on short-sightedness. Only we weren't allowed to call it that anymore, because that wasn't its proper scientific name. It wasn't 'short-sightedness' it was *myopia*. Bauble was *myopic*. And Mum wasn't long-sighted, she was *hyperactive*. No, wait, that's not right. I mean *hyperopic*.

Anyway, hyperactive hyperopic Mum finally got a text from the optician's to say Bauble's glasses were ready for collection. Only she was on an afternoon photo shoot for a walking magazine, so she had to ring Big Mike and ask him to take us instead. Which he did. In fact, he pretty much jumped at the chance. I think he was glad of a break from the boring translation he was working on. Or maybe he just wanted a break from the Mutant Monkey Man impression I was working on: *Blistering banana skins, it's Agent Antelope. And he's got custard. Look out!* It was rather good, though I say so myself.

Big Uncle Mike's not our *actual* uncle of course. Not a proper blood relation, I mean. That's the other one, Mum's brother—also known as 'Little Mike' on account of being a good head shorter than Big Mike. We don't always bother with the Big and Little bits of their names though—somehow everyone knows which one we mean. But it's always Big Mike who keeps an eye on us when Mum's out on a job, because he works from home, turning Swedish books and articles into English. And, as long as we don't make too much noise, he's happy for us to go round there for a few hours.

Little Mike works for some sort of advertising company, but I can never remember what it's called. LTFGM or GMEFT. I don't know. Some random string of letters anyway. It seems like a pretty cool job, apart from having to get the train to London and back every day. He's always getting free stuff too—t-shirts, watches, drinks bottles, all sorts—and he gets to go to some big conference thing in New York every year.

Oh, and you know the new chewing gum advert on telly? The one with the singing pink mouse in a chef's hat, who's slicing onions? That's one of Uncle Mike's. At least, he's the one who came up with the slogan: *Keep Your Choppers Squeaky Clean—Freshen up with Mintereen.* He got loads of free chewing gum when he was working on that, but Mum wouldn't let us have any in case we swallowed it by accident. Shame. We could have done with some Mintereen when we went for our eye tests. That's to say, Mr Garlic-Breath-Puffy-Vampire-Slayer could have done with some. A few packets of the stuff.

Luckily the waiting area whiff had cleared by the time we went in to collect Bauble's new glasses that afternoon. She'd gone for super-bright greeny-yellow ones in the end, which apparently were nothing like Ghandi's or John Lennon's. Nothing like Velma's in *Scooby Doo* either, but she seemed happy enough.

"Gosh," said Big Mike, when she tried them on again to see if they needed adjusting. He pushed his own glasses back up his nose. "They're very erm… striking, aren't they? I'm trying to think what you'd call that colour."

"Luminous Lime?" I suggested. "Bright Bogey?"

Bauble giggled, just as the optician went to take them off her again for some more tightening.

"Sorry," I said. "*Snot* very nice of me, is it?"

That *really* set her off. She was giggling so hard she nearly ended up with a pink nail-polished finger in her eye. Which would have been a bit awkward. *Well, Holly, I'm glad to say that we've corrected the vision in your left eye but I'm afraid I've just blinded you in your right one.*

"Perfect," announced the optician, six squillion adjustments later. "You look just like your dad now."

Bauble froze. Seriously. Her whole body went completely stiff and her lips got stuck in a cartoon-style 'O' shape. My mouth was probably hanging open too but I wasn't shocked so much as excited. Stupidly excited. Having spent so much time thinking about Dad again, dreaming about him, wishing I could talk to Mum about him without setting her off crying or shouting, it seemed too good to be true. If the optician had known him, perhaps I could talk to *her* instead. Not about the black box secrets—I didn't mean that. Just about him. You know, what he was really like. All I needed was to find a way of coming back here on my own, without Mum or Uncle Mike in tow...

Of course I knew talking about Dad wouldn't bring him back. And I knew that collecting random bits of information about him would only make me miss him more. But I didn't care. All that brooding over dark family secrets had brought back feelings I hadn't felt for a long time. Like a dad-shaped hollow inside of me that needed filling. Anything would do—I wasn't fussy. Favourite film. Favourite colour wine gum. Baby nickname. Ketchup or brown sauce with his sausages. Inny bellybutton or outy. Not that I expected the optician to be much help on that last one.

The Uncle Mikes had never been any good when it came to digging up facts. I'd tried before. Lots of times. But they always said it was Mum's place to talk to me about family stuff. That they didn't want to interfere. It was like someone had built a big wall round anything to do with Dad and they were worried they might knock it down by mistake. It didn't matter how silly or trivial my questions were, I always got the same answer:

"Do you know what Dad's favourite pizza topping was?"

"You'll have to ask your mum about that."

"What size shoes did my dad take?"

"Perhaps you'd be better off talking to your mum."

"Did he snore?"

"Hmm. That's probably a question for your mum, don't you think?"

Only it never was. I never asked her anything about Dad. Not once I was old enough to understand, anyway. The thing was, she'd been so much happier the last few years. Properly happy I mean, not just pretending to make me and Bauble feel better. I knew for a fact she didn't need tablets from the doctor anymore, because they'd disappeared out of the bathroom cabinet. And I couldn't even remember when I'd last caught her crying under the pink wishing bow. I liked it that way. I liked *her* that way: happy and chatty. Pretty happy anyway. And *very* chatty. I guess I was scared of opening up old wounds again. Maybe Uncle Mike was too. Maybe that's why *he* went all funny when the optician mentioned Dad.

He seemed very interested in his own feet all of a sudden. Like he'd never seen such a fascinating pair of trainers. "Ah. No. I'm just Bauble's... I mean Holly's... I'm just her uncle," he stammered.

It took me a moment or two to catch up. And then the penny dropped, taking my hopes down with it. The optician didn't know Dad at all, she'd simply assumed Uncle Mike was our father.

"Of course," she said, looking embarrassed, as if she sensed she'd put her foot in it somehow. "Well in that case you look exactly like your uncle in your new glasses! Yes, I can certainly see the family resemblance."

Uncle Mike studied his trainers a bit more. It seemed like we were *all* staring at his shoes. At his muddy laces and the old tomato sauce stain on the tip of his left foot, from when he was making pizzas.

I was waiting for Bauble to set the optician right. To correct her, like she's always correcting me. *But that's impossible*, I imagined her saying. *Because technically we're not family at all…* before reeling off some Baubley fact about humans sharing sixty percent of their genes with fruit flies. That's one of her all-time favourites. But she didn't say anything. At least nothing like that.

"Thank you very much for your help," she whispered. And that was it.

She was quiet all the way home too. Everyone was.

"Tell you what," I said, trying to cheer her up. Or maybe I was trying to cheer myself up. "Why don't we spend this afternoon catching up on our investigation? We could try writing to him—Father Christmas, I mean—and see if he replies."

"Oh. Okay," she said, without much enthusiasm. Anyone would think I'd suggested an afternoon of scrubbing the kitchen floor. With our tongues. "If you want."

7

AGENT ANTELOPE
STRIKES AGAIN

At least we had a proper notebook now. That was one
bit of progress. It was a pretty smart one too, like a
mini folder, with metal clips to hold the pages in, and
different sections with coloured dividers. Bauble had
asked Little Mike—the advertising one—if he had any
free writing pads going spare, and that's what he gave
her. And two pens shaped like sticks of rock from a
company called Beach Living. Shame they didn't *taste*
like sticks of rock.

It turned out I was wrong when I said Bauble had
been too busy to do any investigating. She'd filled in
whole pages on her own while I wasn't looking. There
was even a cover page, with a picture of Santa cut out
of an old Christmas card, and a gold glitter glue frame.
Then came a surprisingly long list called EVIDENCE

FOR DAD BEING FATHER CHRISTMAS. Some of that was stuff she'd already told me about but there were new bits of 'evidence' too, like his name—she seemed to think Nick was short for Saint Nicholas—and the fact that Mum didn't keep any photos of him round the house. *No one ever talks about him* was up there at number three, with 'suspicious secrecy' added in brackets afterwards. Even the cat had made it onto the list:

5. Rudy—short for Rudolph??

Hmm. I'd never really thought about why he was called that. I assumed it was something to do with him being so grumpy. You know, because Rudy sounded a bit like 'rude' and rhymed with moody. That's what we called him when he got all hissy and scratchy: Moody Rudy. But that's not to say it couldn't be short for Rudolph too...

Number seven was new as well: *No evidence of other dating. No new boyfriends.* Ugh. That one made me feel a bit weird. I didn't really want to think about Mum meeting someone new—about her actually kissing someone, outside of Bauble's imagination—

so I jumped right down to the end of the list:

15. He always puts his plate away after he's eaten his mince pie.

"What does that mean?" I asked her. "How would you even know?"

Bauble looked at me over the top of her glasses. She'd put them on especially for our detecting session, though I don't think Sherlock Holmes or Watson ever wore luminous bogey spectacles when they were working a case. Not on the trailer *I'd* seen, anyway.

"You know how we always leave out a mince pie for Santa on Christmas Eve?" she said. "And a glass of sherry? And carrot chunks for the reindeer?"

I nodded. It had been part of our family tradition for as long as I could remember. Right after we finished watching *A Christmas Carol* in our pyjamas. All three of us snuggled up under the special snowman blanket in front of the telly, stuffing our faces with marzipan fruits.

"Well," said Bauble. "He *always* washes up the empty plate and glass when he's finished. He must do, mustn't he? Because they're not there in the morning.

And I know for a fact he doesn't do that when he goes to Chloe Corston's house. He just leaves them next to the fire, with crumbs all over the plate." She wrinkled up her nose like she didn't think much of such sloppy Santa behaviour, even if she *was* his secret daughter. "Chloe brought in a photo of them for January Show and Tell when we were in Reception Class," she explained. "Well, it was a picture of her and her brother opening their Christmas stockings, but I could see the plate and glass right there behind them."

Trust Bauble to remember what was in the background of someone else's photo from years before. I didn't doubt *that* bit for one moment. But I wasn't too sure what the plate business proved exactly. It was a pretty big leap from a couple of clean dishes to an entirely new dad. One who flew reindeer and squeezed down chimneys for a living.

"Oh," I said. She'd clearly given the matter a lot of thought over the last few days, while reading every single book ever written about the human eye, and I was supposed to be cheering her up, not making her feel even worse. So I settled for an 'oh' and flicked on to the next section: EVIDENCE AGAINST DAD BEING FATHER CHRISTMAS. It was completely empty.

"You haven't got much on here yet," I pointed out. Nicely, of course. I could think of plenty of things, just off the top of my head. Like the fact that Father Christmas was an old man. Hundreds of years old. And Mum was only twenty-eight. Yuck! And then there was the small matter of our stockings…

Bauble must have had the exact same thought. "Well," she said. "I *was* going to put down how we don't get any special treatment when it comes to our stockings. In fact, Chloe Corston gets much better stuff in hers. But Santa's not stupid, is he? I mean *Dad's* not stupid. Everyone would guess otherwise. If they all got boring stuff like toothbrushes and satsumas, and we got puppies and robots and entire libraries of books."

"I suppose so…" I said. I was still busy picturing a puppy wriggling around inside my stocking. How cool would that be?

"Anyway," Bauble went on. "I know you don't really believe me. About him being Father Christmas, I mean. So I've started another list for you at the back."

I turned to the last page, and there it was— ALTERNATIVES.

My throat started to sting and my eyes went all prickly as I stared at the list. That's if you can call two things a list:

1. Undercover policeman
2. Spy / Secret agent

There was a third option too, but that had been crossed out:

~~3. He really is dead~~

I so wanted one of them to be true. A spy, preferably. That would be the coolest of all. Think of the amazing gadgets! Cars that shot bullets out of their exhaust pipes. Pens that doubled up as poisoned darts. Mini cameras hidden inside buttons. I felt like crying and giggling all at the same time, as my imagination took over. Dad wasn't dead, he was James Bond! He was West Elphington's answer to Agent Antelope, Mutant Monkey Man's dangerous double-crossing arch enemy. Only he was a good double agent, not an evil one.

The more I thought about it, the more sense it

made. Of course! That would explain why no one ever wanted to talk about him. They were too worried about blowing his cover! *And* it would account for the strange lack of photos round the place. Why there were framed pictures of me and Bauble all along the mantelpiece but none of Dad. It wasn't because they made Mum sad. The wishing bow made her cry all the time and she'd still hung that up where she could see it every day. No, it was because she had to keep his identity a secret. Because no one could know who he was—not even his own children!

"I knew you'd like those ones better," said Bauble, looking very pleased with herself. It was the smiliest I'd seen her all week. "We can investigate them both at the same time if you want. I mean, it was *definitely* Father Christmas I saw Mummy kissing. At least it looked like his head and boots. But I suppose it could have been a disguise. Undercover policeman and spies often have to dress up to avoid detection."

Hmm. If I was looking for a disguise to help me melt into the background, I'm not sure I'd have gone for a bright red hat and bushy beard. But then I thought again about what Bauble had said and realised there was a far bigger mystery to worry about than that.

"Wait a minute, what did you say?" I asked her.

"That they often have to dress up to avoid detection."

"No," I said. "Before then. Something about recognising Father Christmas's head and boots. What about the rest of him?"

Bauble rolled her eyes and sighed, as if the answer should be obvious. "I don't know what the rest of him looks like, do I? I've never seen a picture of him in swimming trunks before."

Huh? I don't know what sort of answer I'd been expecting, but it definitely wasn't that.

"What do you mean, swimming trunks?" My voice had gone all squeaky with surprise.

"You know," said Bauble, impatiently, as if I was acting dim to wind her up. "Like the ones you wear when you go swimming with the school. Only these ones were red to match his hat."

Right. That made everything *so* much clearer. Not.

"Why didn't you tell me any of this before?"

"I must have forgotten," she said, looking shifty. "You're not going to put it on the list, are you?"

"What list?"

"The AGAINST one." She took off her glasses and

folded them up on the table, looking much younger, suddenly, without them. And sadder. "I'm sorry, Noel," she said, softly. "I didn't think you'd believe me, if I told you. *I* wouldn't believe it if I hadn't seen it with my own eyes. But he really was there. In his swimming trunks. And it was *definitely* Mummy he was kissing. I'd have been able to see her even more clearly if I'd had my glasses then, but I'd recognise that spotty cardigan anywhere. Santa had his arms round her like this, and…"

No! Not another re-enactment.

"It's okay," I said, cutting her off before she got started on the grizzly details. "I believe you."

But I didn't.

I was right the first time. It must have been a dream, stray tinsel or no stray tinsel. Father Christmas in swimming trunks? As if!

8

MY DAD,
THE SUPERHERO

Bauble wasn't the only one dreaming about Dad. He'd been making nightly appearances in my head ever since she told me about the kissing stuff. But the dream I had after the swimming trunks revelation was the best (and worst) one yet.

I was sitting at the kitchen table looking at photos of sausages—no people this time, just plain pork and herb bangers—when I heard a loud noise in the back garden. Sort of like a heavy thud, followed by a cat screeching. It wasn't Rudy though, because he was sitting next to me, trying to eat his little chicken biscuits with a spoon. Which for some reason seemed quite normal at the time, even if it did keep slipping out of his paw and landing in the litter tray.

I might have been a bit more scared in real life, in

case the noise was burglars or something, but it didn't even occur to me to be worried in the dream. I went straight over to the back door and stared out into the garden. It was dark outside—really dark, like it was the middle of the night—but somehow I could still see everything. I could see a tall man in red swimming trunks and a Santa hat, with a Mutant Monkey Man pyjama top just like mine. Only bigger, obviously. He had a really cool superhero cape (that was red too) and a mask across his eyes that looked like it was made of meat. Like a big flat steak with two holes cut out for his eyes. It should have been really gross, but it wasn't. Not that it mattered anyway. It was the person behind the mask I was interested in.

"Dad!" I yelled out, banging on the glass with both fists to get his attention. Don't ask me how I knew it was him. I just did. Just like I had in all the other dreams. I wanted to run out to him but I couldn't get the door to open. So I stood there, staring through the glass, willing him to come and get me.

It was working too. He was coming, striding across the garden in what looked like Bauble's old wellies— the orange and white stripy ones with cat ears sticking out the top, that she used to call her Rudy Boots.

He was coming to sweep me up in a giant Dad hug and whisk me away to a new life as his superhero sidekick. I didn't even stop to think about Mum and Bauble. About leaving them behind. I just stood there, willing him on, waving like an idiot.

When he waved back, I saw something shiny in his hand. Something jingly. Mum's house keys! He held them up in the air when he reached the edge of the patio, jangling them around like bells. By then he was so close I could see Mum's metal bird keyring swinging against her two front door keys. I could see the back door key with the blue rubber band wrapped round it (so she'd know which one it was), the garage key with the red rubber band, and the plain brown-banded key for next door (so she could check the mail and water the plants when the Uncle Mikes were on holiday). I could even see the tiny little gold key she kept on there—the mystery one that she couldn't remember what it was for. That's how close he was. Close enough to reach out and touch, if it wasn't for the thin layer of glass between us.

I thought he was going to open the door with them. I thought that's why he was showing me. But he leaned forwards and blew on the window instead, tracing a perfect heart shape with his finger. And then he turned round and walked back down the garden the way he'd come.

"Wait! Come back! Daaaaaaaadddddd!"

That's when I woke myself up, shouting and crying. Bauble heard me all the way through her bedroom wall and came running in to see what the matter was.

"Noel? Are you alright? What's happened?"

I stared at her in confusion, my brain still half-asleep. I couldn't work out what she was doing there at first. Or why my cheeks were all wet. And then it hit me, like an iron fist slamming into my stomach, knocking the breath clean out of my body. Dad had gone. He'd been right there, within touching distance. And then he'd disappeared all over again. It was only a dream. Another stupid dream.

Bauble tried again. "What is it? Does something hurt?"

I shook my head, still crying.

"Was it a nightmare?" she asked.

"Yes. No. I mean, it was a *good* dream. Apart from the very end. And now he's gone…"

Bauble put her arms round me and made the soft

shushy sound that Mum always makes when we hurt ourselves.

"You mean Daddy, don't you?" she whispered. "What did he look like?"

I wiped my eyes on my pyjama top. "I don't know. I didn't really see his face. But I knew it was him."

"Did he have a beard?"

"No. At least I don't think so. Definitely not a big white one anyway. He had an eye mask made of meat though."

She thought for a moment. But not about the mask. "Hmm. Perhaps he shaves it off in the summer. You know, to stop his chin getting too hot and itchy."

"What, at the North Pole? It doesn't ever *get* hot there, does it? Wouldn't all the snow melt?" I had a sudden picture of Father Christmas in a pair of Speedos, water-skiing behind a giant walrus.

"Well, not hot exactly, no. Just less cold," she said. "But I meant when he's on holiday. When he comes to see Mummy." She hugged me even tighter. "Maybe next time he'll stay long enough for us to see him too. Now we're old enough to understand and keep his secret."

She was still clinging stubbornly to her Father

Christmas theory despite all the holes in it. More holes than a Swiss cheese sieve, as Little Mike would say. Perhaps she had a Dad-shaped hollow inside of her too. Maybe that's why she was always stuffing her head full of clever facts and pointless bits of information. She was trying to fill the gap he'd left behind.

The lady at the Post Office once told Mum it was a blessing we were too young to remember Dad. It never felt like that to me though. More like a curse. I'd have given anything to have known him properly. To have actual memories I could turn to when I was feeling lonely, or when all the boys in my class were talking about playing football or going to the cinema with their dads to see the latest *Space Runner* film. What did I have? A 1st birthday card signed 'Daddy', in faded blue ink. The rest of the card was all in Mum's writing but the 'Daddy' and the kisses were definitely his. A 2nd birthday card, also signed 'Daddy', and a battered toy police car that had been his when he was little.

It wasn't very much, was it? Two birthday cards; a toy car that sat in pride of place on my bedside table; and a locked black box, still calling to me from Mum's study. Sometimes it seemed to be saying, *Come and open me, Noel, you know you want to*, and other times it was warning me off: *You know what Mum said. You keep away from me or you'll regret it. There's a reason she hid that key…*

"That's it!" I yelled suddenly, forgetting it was still the middle of the night. Bauble jumped back in surprise, almost toppling off the edge of the bed.

"You think he *will* want to see us next time?" Her voice was a mixture of hope and disbelief. "You think Mummy will let us?"

"No, not that," I said. "The key! I know where it is."

"What key?"

"You know, the one that opens the black box. It was right there in my dream, only I didn't realise it at the time. That's what Dad was doing—he was showing me where to find it." It was the little gold one Mum kept on her keyring. It had to be. I don't know why I hadn't thought of it before. "It's like he *wants* me to open the box," I told her. "Like he's giving me his permission."

Bauble didn't seem quite so convinced. Suddenly Little Miss Scientific was back again, with her fancy long words and spoilsport facts. "More likely it's just your subconscious," she said. "I read an article about dreams the other month and…"

"No." I didn't want to hear any of that. "Dad came to me in my dream for a reason." I didn't mean for my voice to come out so cross but I had to make her understand. I needed it to be true. "He even held up Mum's keys to show me. The missing one was right there, I saw it."

Bauble wasn't giving up either. "But you probably saw it on her keys yourself without realising. And then your brain put the information into a dream along with a load of other stuff and turned it all into a story. But that doesn't mean…"

I opened my mouth to tell her she was wrong, then changed my mind. The last thing I wanted was her running off to Mum and spilling the beans. She'd never really been one of those annoying tell-tale sisters—not like my friend Laurie's little sister—but this was much more serious than the usual stuff I got up to. Accidentally cutting a hole in my bedroom curtains, and spilling an entire bottle of coke on the sitting room carpet, were nothing compared to breaking into that box.

"Maybe you're right," I said, instead. "Perhaps it

was only a dream."

It wasn't though. Dad *wanted* me to open it. And if that little gold key really did turn out to be the right one, then that's exactly what I was going to do.

9

MY DAD, THE SECRET CRIME-BUSTING HERO

Okay, so I knew it wasn't *all* true. I knew some parts of the dream were recycled stuff from another bit of my brain, like Bauble said. Like the weird meat mask. That probably had more to do with Mrs Manzo's sausage snap than anything else. Or worrying about our new freaky meat monster piano teacher. And yes, I *did* know that Dad wasn't really a superhero. At least not one with a cape and magic powers. But what if he was a different kind of hero? What if he really *was* an undercover cop like Bauble suggested, off working with some dangerous criminal gang? And all that stuff about him getting ill and dying—that was just a cover story to explain why he'd gone away in the first place. To explain why Mum used to cry all the time. But now, when he came back for a secret visit—in his swimming trunks and Santa hat?—she was so happy she even started singing.

It made an odd sort of sense if I thought about it hard enough. Which I did. I lay in the dark after Bauble had gone back to bed, thinking about it so hard I got a headache. My eyes went jazzy, like there were flashing white lights dancing behind my eyelids. But I couldn't have switched the thoughts off if I'd tried. I wanted him to be a spy or a special secret policeman, risking his life to bring down the bad guys, just like Bauble wanted him to be Father Christmas. Because that meant he was still alive and one day he'd come back for us. Because it meant the only secrets waiting in the black box were *good* ones. That's where all the paperwork for his real identity was. The stuff that proved he wasn't dead after all. It had to be! And Mum was just worried I'd let the cat out of the bag and put him in danger. That was all. That's why she was so mad at me before. But Dad *wanted* me to look in there and find it. At least the Dad in my dream had wanted me to find it...

It was close to morning when I finally got back to sleep and by then I was too tired for any more dreams. I didn't remember anything else at all, in fact, until my

Mutant Monkey Man alarm clock woke me up at seven o'clock:

"Sweet banana jam!" it blared in my ear. *"I smell a new adventure!"*

I didn't smell anything. Apart from a slightly cheesy whiff coming from my pyjama top, where I'd spilt milk down my front the day before. It was hard to get too excited about that.

"Come on, Dopey Drawers," said Mum at breakfast. "You don't want to be late."

"Huh?" I was staring at the back door, at the place where Dad had drawn a heart in the steamed-up glass. But there was nothing there now. No welly footprints leading up from the garden either.

"You've barely touched your Dino Rocks," said Mum. "Are you sure you're feeling okay?"

"What?" I looked down at my bowl in surprise. I'd sort of forgotten they were there.

"I'm fine," I said. "Just a bit tired, that's all." Make that *very* tired. And more confused than ever. It didn't seem quite so likely in the cold light of day. The whole undercover cop thing, I mean. At least Bauble had a mystery Santa hat and a bit of tinsel to back up her theory. What did I have exactly? Nothing. That's what.

Wanting it to be true wasn't enough.

My head was in a complete muddle all morning. A total brain tangle. I couldn't stop puzzling over my dream, even though it was our first day back at school after the holidays and I had a million other things to think about. Like why had Mum given me Bauble's cheese spread in my sandwiches instead of tuna fish paste? Would the field be dry enough to play football on at lunchtime? And what had happened to our new teacher's hair over the summer? It had definitely been a normal yellow colour when she came into our assembly at the end of July, and now it was a gruesome shade of green. All she needed was a long pointy nose and a few black teeth and she'd be all set for Halloween. Which was funny really, because that was her name—Mrs Witchy. Only when she wrote it up on the whiteboard it turned out she didn't actually spell it like that. 'Mrs Whichey' was much more boring. And when Hannah Scobson put up her hand and asked how she got her hair to look 'so pretty and apple-y' she said it was something to with the chlorine in her holiday swimming pool. Apparently she couldn't recolour it for another two weeks in case it all fell out.

"How cool would that be?" whispered Laurie,

jabbing me in the leg with the rubber end of his *Space Runner* pencil. "She and the headmaster could be shiny-head baldies together."

"What's that, Laurie?" said Mrs Whichey, who'd clearly learnt *his* name already. All the teachers in the school knew who Laurie was, for some reason. "Have you got something you'd like to share with the rest of the class?"

Uh-oh. The last time someone said that to Laurie— a scary supply teacher who seemed to be allergic to children—he pulled out a bag of sour strawberry balls and started offering them round. Which didn't go down very well. Let's just say he had plenty of time to admire the headmaster's shiny-head baldness during lunchtime detention that week. He never got his sweets back either. I reckon the supply teacher sneaked them off to the staff room and scoffed the lot.

"No, miss," said Laurie. "Unless anyone would like to see my verruca?"

Mrs Whichey's face didn't even flicker. "Thank you. That's a very generous offer but perhaps we'll pass on the foot examination for today. I think what people would *really* like to see is you sitting there quietly and getting on with your work. Don't you?"

"Er, yes, miss," said Laurie, sinking back into his chair in defeat. Perhaps he'd finally met his match. It was good to see him again though. His mum was Italian and he and his cousins always spent the summer at his grandparents' villa, somewhere in the countryside near Rome. It sounded amazing. Delicious homemade pasta, giant family Frisbee games in the fields, fishing trips with his *nonno*... It was hard not to be jealous when the most exciting thing we'd done all summer was a trip to a local farm so Mum could photograph some horses. But then maybe it would be Laurie's turn to be jealous when Dad finally came home and everyone found out what a hero he was.

I must have changed my mind about the black box at least ten times before lunch. I was *definitely* going to get hold of that key and see what was inside... No. I couldn't betray Mum's trust like that. She must have a good reason for wanting us to keep out... But I had a right to know. He was *my* dad... Backwards and forwards I went. Yes. No. Yes. No. I was so busy turning it all over in my head—again—that I didn't notice how yucky my cheese spread sandwiches were. I ate them without thinking and hurried outside with the others to play football. At least if I was chasing after the ball I wouldn't have time to worry about keys and clues.

I felt a bit sick later though, when Mrs Whichey told us what our special topic for that term was: 'What Makes Me Me'.

"We'll be learning all about the human body," she said, ignoring the giggling from the back of the class as Laurie pretended to sniff his own armpits, "and exploring our own likes and dislikes. And of course we'll be looking at the importance of family and friends in our lives. With a fun family tree activity to start us all off this afternoon. Doesn't that sound good?" she said, as if she'd just offered us a class trip to Disneyland.

No, I thought. It didn't sound good at all. How could I make a family tree if I didn't have anyone to put on it? Mine would be more like a family twig.

Mrs Whichey handed out the special sheets she'd printed, with boxes for our names at the bottom of the trunk, along with three more for any brothers and sisters, and rows of branches for our parents, aunts and uncles, and grandparents. There were even blank leaf shapes at the very top to add in any great-grandmas and grandads.

"Please, miss," said Hannah Scobson. "What about cousins? Can we put them on as well?"

"What a good idea," said Mrs Whichey. "Maybe you could draw some acorns for them, dangling down underneath whichever auntie and uncle they belong to."

I watched Laurie's overcrowded tree sprout eighteen new acorns. And then I looked back at my bare, wintry stick of a thing: Me and Bauble at the bottom, then Mum (Stella) and Uncle Mike. And the other Uncle Mike. I'd decided against adding Dad onto my tree until I knew the full story. What if Mrs Whichey expected him to turn up for 'Meet the Teacher'? How would I explain that?

"Goodness me, have you finished already?" she asked, heading over for a closer look. "Noel," she added, reading my name off the bottom of my trunk.

I nodded.

"Oh," she said in surprise. "I see. So you don't have any grandparents...?"

"Nope." That's what comes of having orphans for parents. Still, at least she hadn't mentioned the gaping gap next to Mum.

"Gosh. And I see you've got two uncles called

Mike!" She let out a nervous laugh, as if she didn't know what else to say to someone with so few relatives. "How funny! I bet that causes confusion."

"Not really," I mumbled, hoping she'd go away again. Hoping she'd stop staring at my pathetic family stick.

"Lovely," she said, brightly. "Why don't you colour in the empty leaves while you're waiting for the others to catch up? There are some brand new felt pens in the pot on my desk." And with that she moved on to Laurie's tree, whose extra branches reached all the way to the edge of his sheet. "Oooh, *Nonna* and *Nonno*? I'm guessing your grandparents are Italian? Lovely!"

Everyone's trees were lovely. *Lovely, lovely, lovely.* So I went and got a red pen from her desk and started adding some new names of my own. Starting with Nick—I was allowed to change my mind, wasn't I?— right there in the empty leaf next to Stella. Just plain Nick, though. Not *Saint Nick*. I didn't want Mrs Whichey to think I was crazy. And then I gave Dad a dad all of his own, called Frank—mainly because that began with the letter 'F'—and a mum called Felicity, who always made chocolate chip cookies when we went to visit. I even added a picture of one of the cookies hanging off her leaf. And then I did a picture of a superhero next to Dad's name, only the mask made him look like a robber, so I turned him into a giant red squirrel instead. I didn't want Mrs Whichey thinking I'd left him off the tree the first time round because he was locked up in jail.

For one horrible moment, I found myself wondering if he really *might* be in prison. If that was the secret lurking in the black box. What if Dad was a bank robber? Or worse still a murderer? *No!* I shook the thought away again—the sooner I found out the real truth, the better—and carried on with my picture. I knew just the thing to make my tree look less sad and bare. Bananas! And maybe a little Mutant Monkey Man face instead of a great-grandma.

I think I might have overdone it with the bananas, to be honest, especially given they looked more like sausages than fruit. That's why I slipped my family tree into my trouser pocket instead of handing it in at the end of the lesson. The last thing I needed was Mrs Whichey calling Mum into the classroom to complain about me on the first day back. *"And I'm afraid to say Noel ruined his sheet by drawing red sausages all over the branches, as you can see. Not a very good start to the term, is it, Mrs Patermoor?"* And then Mum would see Dad's name next to hers and get all upset again. Or maybe she'd just be cross, which would be even worse. I needed to be on my best behaviour with her from now on—starting with our first piano lesson after school—so she wouldn't suspect anything when I stole the key off her keyring. No, I corrected myself, remembering the bank robber squirrel picture folded away in my pocket. Not 'stole'. When I *borrowed* the key…

10

~~MEAT~~ MEET THE NEW PIANO TEACHER

"What do you know about this Mr March?" I asked Bauble as we sat waiting at the traffic lights. Or was it Mr *Marsh*? Mum was too busy singing along to the radio—more singing!—to hear us.

"Nothing really," she said. "Mummy thought it might be good for us to learn how to play the piano, that's all." We had an old out-of-tune one in the corner of our sitting room, which sort of came with the house. Partly because the lady who lived there before didn't have room for it in her new flat, and partly because it wouldn't go back out through the sitting room door. But no one ever played it because it was always buried underneath photography equipment and piles of ironing. At least it had been until a couple of weeks earlier, when Mum suddenly decided to shift all the piano clutter up onto the landing. Now it was landing clutter instead.

Bauble waggled her fingers up and down an imaginary keyboard. "I think she wanted us to try a few lessons and see how we got on before she paid to get the piano tuner in."

That was pretty much how I remembered the conversation too. "But she didn't mention anything about meat?" I said. "About whether he liked sausages or not…?" That image of Mrs Manzo was still burnt into my brain, refusing to go away.

Bauble wrinkled up her nose. "Sausages? I don't think so. Why?"

"No real reason. I just wanted to be prepared that's all. You know, in case he happened to be wearing any meat products during our lesson…"

"Meat products? What do you mean?"

"Oh, the usual sort of thing," I said, trying to make it into a joke. "Burger ear muffs, maybe, or a tie made out of pork chops…"

Bauble giggled, pressing her fingers into her stomach. "Stop it, you're making me hungry." It turned out there'd been a complete sandwich mix-up—Mum must have got distracted—and Bauble had ended up with my tuna paste ones in her lunchbox instead. Only she hates tuna even more than I hate cheese spread, so she hadn't eaten anything more than crusts and an apple since breakfast. No wonder she was feeling a bit peckish.

I started giggling too. Out of nerves, I think. Half of me was nervous about the piano lesson, about meeting this Mr March in the flesh (ha ha, flesh, get it?), and the other half was nervous about sneaking the key off Mum's keyring without getting caught. Not to mention worrying about what I'd find in the box once I finally got it open.

"Hello," I said, putting on my silliest posh voice. "My name's Mr March. Do you like my pork chop tie? I like to nibble on the end of it while I'm listening to scales. And what about my streaky bacon belt?"

Bauble let out a wild snort of laughter, sending wet droplets spraying out of her nostrils.

"Oh dear, Holly," I said, still in my silly voice. "You've got bogey juice all over my chicken nugget cufflinks. *Snot* very good is it?"

"Stop it," she begged, her whole body shaking up and down. "Before I wet myself."

"What's going on back there, Noel?" said Mum,

eyeing me in her rear view mirror. "Is your sister laughing or crying?"

"A bit of both by the looks of it," I reported, catching sight of the shiny streaks down her cheeks. "But she's fine. Just looking forward to *meat*ing our piano teacher!" And that was it. I was off again too, giggling like a little kid in a tickle competition.

It must have been catching. Even Mum was joining in by the time we got to the piano teacher's house. She laughed out loud when he opened the door and said, "Mrs Patermoor, hello! How nice to see you again." Like he'd just made the best joke ever—maybe Mum was nervous as well.

"Nice to see you too, Mr Marsh," she said, still laughing. But it was definitely Marsh, with an *S H* on the end. Not March. That was a bit of a relief. No meat underwear surprises to worry about. Hopefully.

"And you must be the famous Noel and Bauble," he added. "I've heard all about you. Come in, come in. We're in the second room on the left."

He certainly *seemed* normal enough on first appearances. Not a single slice of salami in sight. Not so much as a hint of ham hidden away under his shirt. He was younger than I'd imagined him too. More like

Mum's age than Mrs Manzo's, with warm brown eyes, a little stubbly beard and a big smile that showed all his teeth.

He led us into what must have been the dining room. Only there was no dining room table, just a couple of wooden chairs, and a battered-looking leather sofa. And, in pride of place under a row of framed certificates and a photograph of some mountains, stood a dark gleaming piano.

"Here she is," he said proudly, smiling his toothy smile and running his hand across the black and white keys like he was stroking them. "Isn't she beautiful? Ten years we've been together now and I love her more every day."

Okay, I thought. *Forget about him being normal.* I had to chew down on the inside of my mouth to stop another attack of the giggles. Mainly because I was already practising impressions in my head to show Bauble later. A funny Italian accent this time—that would work perfectly: *Oh my darrrrrling, I larrrve you so much. Let me kiiiiiss your beautiful white keys.* Yucksters! Anyone would think the piano was his girlfriend! Or a prized pet.

"Oh yes, she's lovely," said Mum, joining in. She

traced her fingers along the polished lid. "Does she have a name?"

A name? What was wrong with everyone all of a sudden? That wasn't a cat they were talking about, it was a bit of wood. Next thing we knew he'd be showing us the piano's squeaky mouse toy and giant litter tray. *Would you like some fiiiish, my daaaarling? My beautiful leeetle pussy-wussykins…*

Mr Marsh looked sheepish and his cheeks turned pink. I'm not surprised to be honest—it *was* all a bit embarrassing. Especially as we'd only just met him.

"Yes," he admitted. "She's called George."

What? But George was a boy's name.

"After Showpan's girlfriend," he added. "That's who *I'm* named after, you see. Showpan."

Showpan Marsh? Really? His parents must have been just as strange as him, I decided.

"Oh yes, of course," said Mum, as if it all made perfect sense. "I should have guessed."

Hmm, I thought, *and* I *should have trusted my earlier suspicions*. This new piano teacher really was bonkers after all. Even without the meat tie and streaky bacon belt.

"Perhaps you'd like to hear a bit of Showpan

before we get started on our first lesson?" he suggested.

Mum's eyes lit up and she nodded and grinned as if he'd just offered her a giant piece of chocolate fudge cake. Which he definitely hadn't. He hadn't even offered her a cup of tea. "Oh yes please, that would be lovely, wouldn't it, kids?"

I'd much rather have had the cake, personally, but I nodded anyway. Seeing as Mum was right there next to me and I was supposed to be on my best behaviour. But then Showpan—Mr Marsh, I mean—sat down and began to play, and Mum might as well have been on the other side of the world. I forgot all about silly impressions and pianos with nonsense names. I forgot about trying to get the key without being caught and what secrets might be waiting for me in the black box. I forgot everything. Dad could have flown through the window in a red cape and matching Santa hat, with an entire roast turkey strapped to each ear, and I'm not sure I'd have noticed. It's like I was hypnotised.

Mr Marsh's hands floated up and down the keys as if his fingers were made of liquid, sending out long rippling waves of notes. Hundreds and hundreds of notes, tumbling over each other like waterfalls. Like ribbons of light streaming off his fingertips... I don't know how to explain it. I just know it was like nothing I'd ever seen or heard before. Beautiful and sad and happy all at the same time. There were fast rushing bits up high and dark heavy bits that caught in your chest and almost made you forget to breathe. I must have closed my eyes while I was listening, because I didn't even notice the music had stopped at first. I was still lost inside the memory of it until I heard Mum and Bauble clapping.

"Wow," said Mum. "That was..." She seemed lost for words. "That was amazing."

She was right about that. "Can you teach *us* to play like that?" I asked him.

Mr Marsh smiled. "Well, we might have to start off a bit simpler to begin with, but you think you'd like to give it a go, do you?"

I nodded. My fingers were itching to try it out for myself.

"I imagine it takes a *lot* of years of practice to get as good as that," said Mum. "But we've all got to start somewhere."

"Absolutely," agreed Mr Marsh. He got up and patted the piano stool. "Tell you what, Noel, you sit yourself down here, and we can make a start right now." He pulled over a couple of the wooden chairs for him and Bauble—one on either side of me—and opened up a book called *Pianoforte Fun*.

"Right," he said, taking a pencil out of his shirt pocket and writing the date over the top of the first tune, 'Middle C Mischief'. "I think we're all set."

Mum settled herself down on the leather sofa with what looked like a photography magazine, and we settled into our first ever piano lesson. I'm not sure there was anything magical about the sounds coming from *my* fingertips exactly. No waterfalls or rushing streams of light. But I liked the feel of the keys when I pressed them down and Mr Marsh said I had a natural technique. I think that was a good thing because he said the same to Bauble when it was her turn. And after three quarters of an hour—though it felt more like ten minutes—we'd both moved way beyond 'Middle C Mischief' and 'Five Fish Fingers'. We could play 'Hot Cross Buns', a tune called 'Ode to Joy' (which you'd probably recognise if you heard it), and 'Jingle Bells'.

Mr Marsh sang along but he did the *Jingle Bells, Batman Smells* version instead, in a really deep voice, and everyone started laughing. Especially Mum—she was laughing the hardest of all.

"So," she said, when we were back in the car afterwards. "What did you make of him then? As a piano teacher, I mean. Do you think you'd like to have lessons with Mr Marsh?"

"Yes," said Bauble, firmly, clutching *Pianoforte Fun* into her chest like a cuddly toy.

"Definitely," I agreed, tapping out another verse of Jingle Bells on my knee. He wasn't an utter nutter after all. A *little* bit crazy maybe, but in a good way.

"Excellent," said Mum, beaming at us in her rear view mirror. "I'll give that piano tuner Mr Marsh recommended a ring first thing tomorrow now I know you're both keen."

She rattled on about something to do with broken strings and a wonky pedal, but I stopped listening after a bit. Now that our lesson was over, I was back thinking about the black box again. About what might be waiting inside. Tonight was the night, while Mum and Bauble were busy watching their baking show. That gave me an hour to find the key and get to the bottom of it all. Sixty whole minutes. What could possibly go wrong?

11

WHAT'S NEW, PUSSY CAT BURGLAR?

Did I mention the row of wishing bows in my bedroom doorway? I wished on every single one of them that evening—twice—as the time for *Baking Britain* drew nearer and nearer. *Please let it be the right key. Please don't let me get caught. Please let it be something good inside the box.* But the more I wished, the more nervous I got, so I headed back down to the sitting room and had another practice of 'Ode to Joy' to help pass the time. It was more like 'Ode to Earache' on our out-of-tune piano though. No wonder the man who wrote it went deaf. Beethoven, that's what his name was—though you say it like 'Bate', not 'Beet'. Mr Marsh told us all about him. He even drew a little cartoon Beethoven in the piano practice notebook he gave me. Bauble got a snowman picture in hers, next to 'Jingle Bells', which she thought was 'brilliant'.

"Mr Marsh is so cool," she kept saying on the way home. "He's really funny, too!" I think it's fair to say she liked him. "And he's *amazing* at playing the piano…" In fact, I think it's fair to say she liked him a lot.

"It's lovely that you're so keen to practise," said Mum, sticking her head round the sitting room door. Though judging by the look on her face she didn't find my playing *that* lovely. "But do you think you could give it a rest now? Bauble and I want to watch *Baking Britain*."

Sweet Banana Jam! It was time!

"Why don't you watch it with us? You might even enjoy it. They're doing superhero-themed party cakes today. And Battenburgs."

"Er, no thanks." I liked *eating* cakes as much as anyone. I liked making them too, mainly because I got to lick out the bowl afterwards. But I wasn't too bothered about watching other people make them. Especially not when I had a life and death undercover operation waiting for me in the next room. Dad's life or death, that was. Not mine, hopefully, unless I got caught and Mum went even more nutso than last time...

"I've got some homework to do," I lied. Actually I did have homework so that wasn't technically a lie. Mrs Whichey wanted us to write a poem about what made us special. "Is it alright if I use your computer?" I added, in a moment of sheer genius. That would give me the perfect alibi for being in Mum's study. Maybe Bauble wasn't the only super brains in the family after all.

"Of course," said Mum. "Just let me close down my work, then it's all yours."

I waited until they were both settled on the sofa. Until the theme tune to *Baking Britain* came booming through the wall. And then I sneaked back out of Mum's study, tiptoeing past the sitting room, and along the hall to the front door. There were Mum's keys, hanging on the hook under the light switch, to remind her to lock the door behind her when she went out. And there was the little gold one, like in my dream.

I pulled the cuff of my school jumper down over my left hand to muffle the noise, and grabbed hold of the keys through the stretched-out wool. Then I eased the gold one right round the keyring to the bit where the metal split, wriggling it free. No problem. I was surprisingly good at this. A natural spy, like Dad. When he wasn't being an undercover cop that was, or a caped superhero slash Father Christmas. Or locked away in prison like a criminal. I'd know soon enough which was the real one though. If he really was still out there somewhere. No more relying on dreams and imagination...

I eased the keys back onto their hook, counting to five in my head to make sure no one had heard, and then retraced my steps to the study. My feet were silent but my heart was noisy as anything, thumping away behind my ribs. I couldn't quite believe I was doing it. That I was actually going through with it this time. But there I was, with the 'borrowed' key in my pocket, pushing old photography magazines to one side and reaching onto the shelf for the famous black box. Like a proper secret agent. Or a cat burglar. Though a burglar would probably have checked out the scene of the crime a bit better beforehand...

I pulled out one pile of magazines after another, but there was nothing behind them anymore. The box was gone. *Holey Sleigh Bell Slippers!* This couldn't be happening. Only it was. Mum must have moved it somewhere more secure after she caught me with it last time. As if she didn't trust me.

No, no, no! Why would she do that? How could she have guessed I'd come looking for it again? That I was the kind of sneaky son who lied to her face and went behind her back when she'd told me to keep away? I tried not to panic. After all, I still had fifty-two minutes left. Plenty of time to find where she'd re-hidden it. I mean, it wasn't exactly the smallest of boxes. There were only so many places it could be.

I worked my way along all the shelves in turn, going as quickly and tidily as I could. Pulling things out, checking behind for a tell-tale glimpse of black metal, and then pushing them back in again. I looked under her desk, round her desk and behind her desk. I even pulled out the drawers in case it had magically shrunk enough over the last week to fit in the little hollow space behind. But other than a couple more chocolate wrappers and a topless photo of the greengrocer, with a wig made out of grapes, there was nothing there.

The Toffee Cruncho wrappers had given me an idea though. The wardrobe! I remembered how long it had taken Mum to find the box of chocolates Dad had stashed away in there. Perhaps *that* was her new hiding place.

I listened for a moment at the door, to make sure the coast was still clear:

"And now let's see how Karen's getting on with her Batman Banana and Chocolate Tower…"

"Wow, that looks amazing," said Mum and Bauble, in unison.

Perfect. I checked the key was still safely tucked away in my pocket and hurried up to Mum's bedroom. It felt even worse than going through her desk—even more private somehow—but I knew if I chickened out now then that would be it. This was a one-time only operation. It had to be, because my nerves couldn't take going through it all again.

Rudy was curled up on the end of Mum's bed, looking very pleased with himself. He knew he wasn't allowed up there but he didn't jump down when he saw me coming like he normally would. Maybe he sensed that I wasn't supposed to be there either. That I was up to even more mischief than him.

"Shh," I whispered, as I crept past. "Pretend I'm not here."

He rolled onto his back and started purring, waiting for me to tickle his tummy. Stupid cat.

"Sorry, Rudes. Not now. I'm on a mission." Thirty-seven minutes left, and counting.

Mum's wardrobe was as much of a muddle as her desk had been, with a thick curtain of clothes dangling down from the over-filled hanging rail, and a sea of shoe boxes, scarves and more old magazines rising up from the floor. Finding anything in there would be an achievement, but at least she wouldn't notice I'd been poking around in her stuff.

Nothing. At least nothing box-shaped. Which just left the high shelf at the very top. I couldn't even *see* up there though, let alone reach. Hmm. Something to stand on—that's what I needed.

I grabbed the pillows off Mum's bed and threw them into a pile in front of the wardrobe. And that's when I saw it. Or rather, that's when I didn't see it. The wrapping paper from Dad's box of chocolates was gone. When did she stop sleeping with that under her pillow? There was something else in its place now instead... A familiar looking postcard of a cartoon robin, with *'My Christmas came early this year! F x'* written underneath.

No time to think about that now though. About why she was sleeping with F's postcard under her head instead of Dad's glittery gold paper. I stacked the pillows up into a wobbly tower and clambered to the top. Only they sank down under my weight, leaving me grasping at thin air.

Come on, think! Less than half an hour to go and I was still no closer to getting inside that box. No closer to finding it. What I *really* needed was to magically grow another thirty centimetres, but not even Mutant Monkey Man could manage that. He shrank once, that time he got attacked by evil reducto-bots, but I'd never seen him get any bigger. Mind you, he could probably swing over on the dangly light fitting and scoop the black box off the shelf with his super-strong tail. While peeling a banana with his feet most likely. What a show off.

I didn't have a super-strong anything, which ruled out the storage-seat kitchen chairs. My chances of lugging one of those monsters up the stairs without banging into the bannisters and giving the game away were tiny. Time was racing away from me and I still didn't know for sure if the box was even there. But maybe if I rolled up the duvet and piled the pillows on the end of the bed I could at least *see* up onto the shelf…

"Sorry Rudy, you'll have to move."

It was a bit unsteady, but it worked. From the top of my teetering tower I could see more or less everything. The hats, the shoe boxes marked 'photos', the old Lego tub (I wondered where that had gone), and a black metal corner, peeking out from a tangled nest of tights. *Gotcha!* I glanced down at the gap between the bed and the wardrobe. Not too far at all. I could probably reach from there. One hand on the side of the wardrobe to keep myself steady and another to ease the box out from behind the tangle of tights. They looked like black snakes, keeping guard over the hidden treasure.

I leaned forwards, wobbling like crazy as my right hand reached for the wardrobe frame. So far so good. I took a moment or two to steady myself—*deep breath now, you can do this*—and then moved on to the tricky bit. The *really* tricky bit. To be honest, I didn't even know how I was going to do it with only one free hand. But I made a start, easing the box out at the bottom corner with my fingers, tugging at the knotted tights in the hope they might bring it out with them. And it was working too. The box was halfway over the edge of the shelf already. The answers I'd been looking for were literally at my fingertips. And then Rudy went and ruined everything.

Okay, so I might have lost my balance a tiny bit and stepped sideways off the pillows onto his paw. But there was no need for him to go all nutso on me. He was fine. And I'd have been fine too if he hadn't turned into a hissing ball of razor claws and fur, attacking my ankle like it was a runaway rat. The pain and shock hit me in a double wave, sending me reeling. Then the pillow tower toppled out from under my remaining foot and I slammed forwards into the hard frame of the wardrobe with an almighty crash. I must have twisted as I fell, catching a flash of black metal and writhing snakes as the box came slamming down after me. And then everything went dark.

12

MY DAD, THE LEGEND

I don't know who got there first, but it was Bauble I remembered seeing when I opened my eyes. You know the saying 'as white as snow'? That's what she looked like. Not just pale-faced, but proper white. Like a sheet of paper. A shaking one.

"Wake up, Noel," she kept saying, even though I already had. Perhaps she was crying too hard to see. "Please wake up."

And then Mum's face was there too. She was pretty white-looking as well.

"Out the way, sweetheart," she said. "I need to check he's okay. You run and get the Uncle Mikes, there's a good girl. And don't worry. He's going to be fine."

Was I? That was good. Because my skull felt like

someone had split it in half. And then stuffed hot burning coals down the gap in the middle.

"Noel," said Mum. I think she might have been crying too but I was trying not to look at her eyes. She must have seen the box. Seen the mess I'd made going through her stuff. She must've guessed what I'd been doing up there. "Can you hear me?"

I nodded. At least I tried to but the slightest movement sent fresh shooting pains through my head.

"Harrrgghhh," I said, which was as close to a 'yes' as I could manage.

"Does anything hurt? Can you still feel your legs?"

That was a trickier one. How could I answer two different questions at the same time? "Harrgghhhh. Haarrgghhhh." *Yes it does* and *yes I can.*

"Okay, we're going to wait for the Mikes to get here. They'll know what to do. Just lie still for now. Everything's going to be fine."

She didn't *sound* cross. Perhaps that would come later, once she realised I wasn't about to pass out again. Or die. At least I hoped I wasn't about to do either of those. I *did* want to see Dad again—more than anything—but in this life, not the next one. I could just make out the drooping pink tail of his wishing bow out the corner of my eye. At least Mum hadn't got rid of *that* as well.

Please let me be alright, I wished, even though I wasn't standing underneath it. It was worth a try. *And please let Mum forgive me.*

I did a mental check round my body while we were waiting for Bauble to get back with the Uncle Mikes. Head? Still attached to my neck but too painful to move. Shoulders? Left one hurting, right one more or less okay. Same with my arms. What about legs? They seemed fine. Toes? Yep, I could feel them too. I could even waggle them up and down inside my socks. And then I risked another look at Mum. She wasn't quite so pale now but she was still crying. Her cheeks had gone streaked and slimy where the tears had run into her face cream. And her mouth had sort of disappeared, as if she'd sucked her lips in too tight with worry.

"Ahm orrryy," I told her, as a wave of wooziness swept across the back of my eyes. *I'm sorry.* I might have been the one lying on the floor with a broken head—that's what it felt like, anyway—but I knew I wasn't the only one hurting. The only one who was scared. She'd be alright when the Uncle Mikes got there though. That's what I told myself. They were good in a crisis. Little Mike always knew exactly what to say to calm Mum down when she was in one of her flaps. And Big Mike used to be a St John Ambulance cadet. He was the one we always went to with cuts and burns and mini medical emergencies.

"This is all my fault," Mum whimpered, wiping at her cheeks with shaking hands.

How did she work that out? It was Rudy's fault, not hers. And mine of course. I was the one who went pillow mountaineering behind her back when I was supposed to be doing my homework.

"I should never have let it come to this," she said, shaking her head and sending tiny tear droplets spraying down onto my face. "Oh Noel, I'm sorry. I should have told you a long time ago."

Told me what?

"The thing is," she blurted out, "your dad's not who you think he is."

The mist behind my eyes cleared again. I knew it! He was alive! He really *did* have a secret identity. Which one was it though? Policeman? Spy? Swimming-trunked Santa? Perhaps he had a different name too—something beginning with 'F'.

"He loved you so much, he really did, but…" She broke off, crying harder now.

But he had to go away. I finished the sentence for her in my head. I wanted to tell her it was alright. That Bauble and I had already guessed, even if we couldn't quite agree on his job. He was alive, though. That was the main thing.

"But you've got a right to know the truth," Mum said, the words hiccupping out of her in wet messy sobs. "Especially with Dad gone." She stroked a stray bit of fringe off my forehead. "You've got a right to know who your real father is."

What? Something about that wasn't right. Dad *was* my real father.

Wasn't he?

The bedroom door burst open and Bauble stumbled back into the room.

"They're coming," she panted. "They're on their way. Is he alright? Why's he gone so pale?"

I *felt* pale. I felt like everything I'd ever known— the whole world—had been sucked out of me while I lay there. I kept playing the same words over and over in my head, *Dad gone… a right to know who your real father is…* but I couldn't get them to make any sense.

Not any *good* sense, anyway.

"Now then," said Little Mike, making his voice extra jolly as he followed Bauble into the bedroom. "What's been going on in here?" He moved the upturned black box out of the way and knelt down on the other side of my head. "It's not Halloween until next month, Noel. You don't want to be frightening everyone just yet." He leaned in closer, flashing me an upside-down grin. "How are you feeling, mate?"

Like someone had pulled my insides out and stamped on them. Like someone had unstitched my brain and taken out every single thought I'd ever had and chopped it up into tiny pieces.

"Harrgghhhh." I told him. "Maaa head haarrts."
Not my real dad.

"Your head hurts? I'm not surprised," said Uncle Mike. "You stay there while Mike checks you out— he's on his way over now, as soon as he's finished on the toilet—and then we'll…"

No. I didn't want to stay there. I wanted to go back in time and pretend none of this had ever happened. I pulled myself up into a sitting position, trying to ignore the black swimmy feeling in my head. But there was no ignoring the thoughts that came with it—the same dark thoughts swirling round and round my brain. *He's not my dad... Never was... Why didn't anyone tell me? Dad's not my dad... Never was... What happened to my real dad?*

"Hey, steady now," said Uncle Mike.

"Ahm fine," I said, reeling sideways into the end of Mum's bed. She lunged forwards to catch me.

"Leb me go."

But Mum held on tighter than ever, hugging me into her chest as a fresh trickle of tears dripped into my hair.

"What's wrong?" asked Bauble. "Why's everyone crying?" I hadn't even realised I *was* crying until then. "Is he going to be okay?" Her voice had gone all wobbly too. Like she might be about to join in again.

"Your brother's going to be fine, sweetheart," said Uncle Mike. "Everything's going to be fine." He paused. I couldn't see what was going on but I could almost feel him and Mum exchanging looks over my head. "I think he could do with some frozen peas on that lump of his though. Why don't you go and fetch him some from the freezer?"

"Thank you," whispered Mum, as Bauble hurried back downstairs.

"I don't know what's been going on here," said Uncle Mike. His voice had lost its singsong brightness. "But I can guess. Now's not the best time though. We need to make sure you're okay first, Noel. And we need to think about Bauble."

Mum nodded. I could feel her head bobbing up and down above mine.

I didn't say anything. I closed my eyes against the whole sorry mess and buried myself deeper into her chest. If I could have closed my brain off I'd have done that too. *Please let this be a dream*, I asked the wishing bow in the doorway. It was like Dad had died all over again. Only this time he'd taken all my stupid fantasies with him. This time he was so dead I'd lost him altogether.

13

THE SMELL OF ~~HOSPITALS~~ SALMON

Voices came and went over my head.

"Noel, can you hear me?" said Uncle Mike. Big Mike, I mean. He must have finally finished on the loo. "Open your eyes for me, there's a good boy."

I did as he asked, grunting by way of an answer. *Go away. Leave me alone.*

"We need to get him down to A&E and make sure he's alright…" That was Mum again. "He *will* be alright won't he? Or do I need to call an ambulance?"

"No, no need for that. What's that you've got there, Bauble? Frozen peas? Perfect."

"I couldn't find the peas. Sorry. It's frozen fish pie mix."

"I'm sure that'll do the trick. Thank you. And don't look so worried. Everything's going to be okay."

No it's not. Nothing's ever going to be okay again.

"That's quite a bump you've got on your head there, Noel. I'm going to put this er... this handy mixture of frozen cod, smoked haddock and salmon chunks on to help with the swelling. It might be a bit cold at first..."

A bit cold? Try freezing.

"To be honest, I'm not sure I'm in a fit state to drive." That was Mum talking. "Can one of you take us?"

"Of course," said Big Mike. "You go, Mike. I'll stay here with Bauble."

"Did you hear that, Noel? Your mum and I are going to pop you down to the hospital to get you checked out. Nothing to worry about though—it's just to be on the safe side. Make sure everything's still in the right place!"

"Why can't I go with you?" said Bauble. "Please, Mummy. I want to come."

"No, sweetheart." That was Big Mike again. "They could be there ages waiting to see a doctor and you've got school tomorrow. Besides, I need someone to stay and keep me company. Help me out with that big bar of fruit and nut chocolate I've been hiding from your uncle…"

Perhaps I drifted off after that. Perhaps I stopped listening. Or maybe that's when the little voice in my head—the one going *If Dad's not your real dad then who is?*—stopped whispering and started shouting instead. I did my best to block it out, to block *everything* out, and before I knew it I was halfway down the stairs in Little Mike's arms. Being carried like a baby, with Mum and the bag of frozen fish chunks following behind.

The television was talking to itself in the sitting room as we passed but I couldn't tell if it was still *Baking Britain* or not. What did it matter anyway? My plan to dig out all the family secrets in the time it took to bake a Batman cake already belonged to a different lifetime. That was the old Noel. The one who made up stupid stories in his head about a man who wasn't even his dad.

I thought Mum would tell me more on the way to the hospital, now we were on our own again—not counting Uncle Mike, who must have known it all already. But she hardly said a word. She sat next to me in the back of the car, stroking my hair and making soft shushy sounds, leaving all the talking to Uncle

Mike. Not proper talking though—not 'So Noel, how do you feel now you know we've been lying to you all these years?'—just general chatter, to try and take everyone's mind off what had happened. Off where we were going.

I let it wash over me like a background stream of sounds: *blah blah funny programme on telly last night, new advertising campaign at work blah blah blah-dee blah-dee blah…* It was easy enough to ignore. Much easier than the picture of Dad in his wellies and cape, with that stupid meat mask over his face. I kept thinking about the keys he'd shown me in my dream. It was like he *wanted* me to know the truth. Like he was tired of pretending to be someone he wasn't. Of pretending to love me. And the heart he'd drawn on the window? That must have been for someone else. For Mum.

I hardly had to wait at all when we got to the hospital. Perhaps they took one look at Mum's white face and bumped us up the queue before she passed out in the waiting room. Or perhaps it was the smell of defrosting fish chunks that did the trick. Either way, it felt like my bum had barely touched the seat before a smiley nurse arrived to help me into a wheelchair.

(Not sure what that was for exactly—my legs were fine.) And then we were off, speeding away down the corridor, with Mum and Uncle Mike in hot pursuit.

◆ ◆ ◆

"I don't think there's any cause for alarm," said Dr Pashka, after she'd finally finished prodding and poking and shining her torch in my face. "Though I'd like you to keep a careful eye on him over the next forty-eight hours or so. Any concerns or worries, then bring him straight back and we'll have another look at him."

"Of course," said Mum. "Thank you."

Dr Pashka turned her attention back to me. "And as for you, young man, you need to take a bit more care. No more throwing yourself off the furniture! You gave Mum and Dad a nasty fright there."

"He's not my dad," I said, almost spitting the words. "I don't even know who my dad is." Mum had been lying to me all along. *Everyone* had been lying to me. All those times I'd lain in bed, clutching Dad's old police car into my chest to try and remember him. Every time I'd traced my finger along the 'Daddy' in my birthday cards… all those hundreds of wishes underneath the wishing bows. It had all been one big fat lie.

"I'm so sorry," said Mum, but I couldn't even bring myself to look at her. It turned out she wasn't talking to me, anyway. It was the doctor she was apologising to. "It's been quite a night, one way or another," she explained. "We're all a bit on edge."

"Well I'd recommend taking it easy for the next couple of days if you can," said Dr Pashka. "Plenty of rest, that's the best thing for Noel now, and maybe something for the pain if and when he needs it." She smiled at me and I felt kind of bad for being rude. It wasn't *her* fault. "And as I say, any more worries, then bring him straight back here. It's always better to be on the safe side."

"We will do. Thank you," said Mum, already heading for the door as if she couldn't wait to get out of there. Perhaps hospitals reminded her of when Dad died. I mean, when not-Dad died.

"Don't forget your fish pie mix," called Dr Pashka. "*Please* take it with you. I think it's starting to swim."

"Perhaps we should talk about this properly now we know you're okay," said Mum, once we were back in the car. "If you want to that is. You must have a lot of questions."

Yes. No. I didn't know what I wanted.

"I always meant to tell you," she went on, taking my confused half-nod, half-shrug as a 'yes'. "When I thought you were old enough to understand." So not yet then. Because I was still a million miles away from understanding. "But I didn't want it to change how you felt about your dad."

"My *real* dad, you mean? How can it? I don't even know who he is."

Mum took hold of my hand and squeezed it tight. "Dad *was* your real dad, Noel. Just not biologically, that's all. And he always will be. He loved you more in the short time you had together than some people get loved in a whole lifetime. As for your birth father, he's… well he's a name on your birth certificate, that's all. He's been gone a long time now."

"Is he dead too then?"

Mum shook her head. "No, sweetheart. Not as far

as I know. But we're not exactly in contact. I haven't seen him since I first found out I was pregnant."

"Does he even know about me?" Stupid question, I thought. Of course he didn't. Otherwise he'd have been there wouldn't he? Cheering me on at football matches with all the other dads. Clapping at school assemblies and taking me to see the latest *Space Runner* film. "Why didn't you tell him?" I said, yanking my hand away.

Mum started crying again. Like *she* was the one who'd been lied to all these years.

"Finn knew all about you," she said. "I told him we were going to have a baby and… and… well, that's why he left. I'm sorry, sweetheart, but if you want the truth…" She pulled out a scrunched up tissue and blew her nose. "We were both very young… too young…"

"So Bauble's not even my real sister?"

"Of course she is," said Mum. "She'll always be your sister. Having different dads doesn't change that. It doesn't change anything."

"Are you sure this is a good idea?" interrupted Uncle Mike. I'd forgotten he was even there. "Having this conversation right now, I mean. It's an awful lot for Noel to process and Dr Pashka said he should be taking things easy."

"She also told him not to go throwing himself off any more furniture," sniffed Mum. "And maybe if I hadn't been such a coward last week—if I'd sat him down and talked about it then—he wouldn't have ended up in A&E in the first place. Better he hears it from me now than risk something like this happening again. Right, Noel?"

I didn't say anything for a long time. I was still trying to get my head round it all. The dad who *did* love me wasn't my dad. Only Bauble's. But he never got to love her like he loved me because he died before she was born. And my real dad—Finn—he was still alive but didn't give a stuff about me.

"Yes," I said at last. "I *do* want to talk about it." But I didn't actually do any talking. I just listened.

Once Mum got started there was no stopping her. She was like a shaken-up bottle of lemonade with the lid taken off—only it wasn't bubbles fizzing out of her, it was a whole other lifetime of secrets. She told me how the lady who ran the care home where she and Uncle Mike grew up had been super-strict (she made her sound like the evil prison guard in *Mutant Monkey Man and the Fortress of Steel*), and how lonely she was after Uncle Mike went off to university. I'm not surprised. It was bad enough growing up without a dad—what must it have been like without any parents at all? Imagine if it was only me and Bauble, and then she went away too… No. I didn't want to imagine that.

Mum told me how everything changed when Finn arrived at the home. How she'd fallen in love with him—with his big brown eyes and wild ways—and wanted to run away with him. She *did* run away with him in fact only, when he found out I was on the way, he kept on running. Without her. And because she couldn't face going back to the home, pregnant, she went to live with Uncle Mike, and Big Mike, instead.

"I don't know what I'd have done if it wasn't for them," she said. "What *we'd* have done. They helped me get a place at the local college to finish my A-levels. They took me to all my hospital appointments. Held my hand through the birth. Got up in the middle of the night to change your nappy when you were crying…"

"That's what families are for," piped up Uncle Mike. "Although some of your more explosive nappies were pushing it a bit as I remember," he added, chuckling to himself.

"And then when you were three months old, a new neighbour moved in next door." Mum stopped to blow her nose again, but I had a feeling I already knew who this neighbour would turn out to be. And I was right. "Nick," she added, smiling as she said his name. "It was love at first sight. I mean, he fell in love with *you* at first sight. Oh Noel, he really *was* your dad. In every way that mattered. And he always will be."

14

DEAR FATHER CHRISTMAS

I hardly slept at all that night, though I pretended to every time Mum came in to check on me. My head was still spinning—not from where I'd hit it, but from all the new information whirling round my brain. I'd gained a brand new dad I never even knew existed. But I'd lost half a sister in the bargain. Maybe that's why Bauble and I were so different. Because we were only half-brother and sister. That might explain why she ended up with all the family geniusness—I'm not sure that's even a word—and I got all the er… well, nothing really. Unless you counted being able to balance a spoon on the end of my nose for one minute and thirty-seven seconds.

I guessed I probably took after my real dad instead. I might not have many 'wild ways' exactly—snotty tissues under the bed was about as wild as it got—but I did have brown eyes. And… well, I didn't know what else. Because apart from his first name that was all Mum had told me about him. Brown eyes, wild ways, and not wanting me. Oh yes, and young, that was the other thing. *Too* young, she said. As if that was some kind of excuse for turning his back on us…

Sleep must have caught up with me eventually, because I dreamt Bauble was locked away in a high tower and the only way she could fit through the window to escape was if I cut her in half with my laser sword. It wasn't a very nice dream and I was glad to wake up and find her sitting on the end of my bed. Both halves of her, top *and* bottom, though it was the top half doing all the talking. Her bottom half does a pretty good job of keeping its thoughts to itself, apart from when we have sprouts for dinner.

"At last! I thought you'd *never* wake up," she said, pouncing on me through the duvet like Rudy does, and squeezing her arms round my waist. "Mum's still fast asleep too, but I saw Uncle Mike on his way to work this morning and he said you're going to be fine." She stopped cuddling my tummy and turned her attention to my head instead. "You *are* going to be alright, aren't you? I wanted to stay up and wait for you last night but Big Mike wouldn't let me. We had about four squares of chocolate and one game of Chase the Lady, then he put the cards away and packed me off to bed. He said that's where you'd be going as soon as you got in as well. To recover. He said I wouldn't be missing anything."

"No," I agreed. "You didn't." That was the last thing Mum said to me when we got home. *Promise me you won't tell Bauble. Not yet.* And even though I didn't think it was fair—even though I thought she had a right to know as well—I found myself slipping into the lie without trying.

"Will you be going to school today?"

"Nope. Two days off. The doctor at the hospital says I've got to take it easy."

"Ah, poor you," said Bauble. She probably meant it too. Most people would jump at the chance to lie on the sofa watching telly all day. Mutant Monkey Man Marathon here we come! But not my little sister. Half-sister, I mean. She'd be too worried about missing out on something in lessons. Some juicy fact that she hadn't come across before, or a new way of multiplying long strings of numbers together in her head. "Still," she added. "At least you're okay. That's all that matters. I thought you were dead when I saw you lying there like that. What were you trying to do?"

That was a tricky one. "Experimenting," I said. "You know, with pivot points and those fulcrum thingies you were reading about the other week." *Right before you dropped the Dad-bomb.* "Only it turns out you can't really balance on a big pile of bedclothes and pillows—I can't anyway—so it was all a bit of a fail."

She wasn't convinced. "Don't be silly. It was something to do with that box, wasn't it? The one you found in Mummy's study."

It looked like my cunning cover story was a fail too.

"I saw it there after Uncle Mike carried you downstairs," she went on, in full detective mode. "Did you manage to open it? Did you see what was inside?"

"No," I said, truthfully. "It sort of fell on me before I had a chance." My head gave a sudden throb of pain at the memory and I wriggled out of bed to examine my wound in the wardrobe mirror. There wasn't much to see though. Just a disappointingly small pink bump peeping through my hair. And a vaguely fishy smell on my fingers afterwards.

"Oh," said Bauble, as if she'd been hoping for a

different answer. I'm not sure what exactly. Photographic evidence of Mum at the North Pole, maybe? A copy of Dad's sleigh driving licence? "So what next? Will you try again? Do you want *me* to try?"

I pretended to think about it. "Perhaps we should call it a day and go back to the original plan. You know, write to him and see what he says." I meant Father Christmas of course, but as I was saying the words out loud I found myself thinking about Finn. About what would happen if I wrote to *my* father? Last night he seemed like the bad guy, but this morning... Well, things always seem better in the morning, don't they? Perhaps he *would* want to know me now I was older. I mean, a baby was one thing—no wonder he found that idea a bit scary—but almost-eleven-year-old boys were no trouble at all.

"I already have," said Bauble, grinning. "I'll go and get it."

I was so caught up in my own thoughts I hardly noticed she was gone. Finn would be that much older too now. Too old to still be running away. And maybe he'd changed his mind since then, only he didn't know where to find me because he and Mum had lost touch...

"Here it is." Bauble was back, waving a green

piece of notepaper in my face. "I wrote it from both of us. Is that alright?"

"Of course," I told her, forcing myself to concentrate. "Let's have a look then."

Dear Father Christmas,

I hope you don't mind us writing to you so early, but this isn't a normal letter. It's us—Bauble (Holly) and Noel! You were at our house a week ago, kissing our mum (Stella Patermoor). I wasn't spying on you, honestly, I just happened to see you when I came downstairs to get my book. It was hot that night and I was having trouble sleeping. You must have been hot too because you were wearing swimming trunks.

Please don't worry, we haven't told anyone you were here and Mummy definitely hasn't. In fact, she must be the world's best secret keeper because we never guessed until last week. Not even with our Christmassy names (I'm guessing you helped her choose those)! But we're really good secret keepers too and you can totally trust us. If you really are our dad we promise we won't tell another living soul. Cross our hearts. We don't want special treatment or anything when it comes to presents, we just want to meet you properly and get to know you. I think that would make Mummy happy too. It would be nice to be a proper family, even if it's only for a few days a year. I know how busy you are.

Please write back and let us know if you really are our dad. That way Mummy won't have to break any promises and I can prove to Noel that I'm right!

Lots of love,

Bauble and Noel xxxx

P.S. Thank you for tidying up the dishes every year after you've had your mince pie and sherry.

P.P.S. I'm sorry I didn't eat the satsuma you gave me last Christmas. I think I left it too near the radiator or something because it looked a bit mouldy. (The sugar mouse had gone all sticky too but that was delicious.) Thank you for the history magazines by the way—they were brilliant!!!!

P.P.P.S. I know I said we didn't want special treatment when it comes to presents, but I would <u>really</u> like a new world atlas. Ours is a bit out of date now. Thank you!! xxxxxxxxx

"So?" said Bauble. "What do you think? Is it okay?"

I didn't know what to say. She looked so hopeful.

"It's fine," I told her. "I mean, it's great. But you mustn't be too disappointed if you're wrong…"

She shook her head. "I know what I saw, Noel. And if it turns out it wasn't actually him… well, it's better to know, don't you think? At least then we can rule him out of our investigation. What is it Sherlock Holmes says?"

"Over to you, Doctor Snotson?" That was a guess. "Has anyone see my pipe? Listen to your awesome big brother because he's wiser than you think?"

Bauble wrinkled up her nose as if she was trying to sniff out the right memory.

"When you have eliminated the impossible," she said, "whatever remains, *however improbable*, must be the truth."

"Of course. That would have been my next guess…" I handed her back the letter.

"Have you got a pen I can borrow?" she said. "Perhaps we should put something about that at the bottom."

I fetched her my stick of rock pen and she added

in an extra bit at the end. In very small writing because she'd nearly reached the end of the page:

P.P.P.P.S. If it wasn't you kissing Mummy in the kitchen please let us know as soon as possible. There's a small chance it might have been an imposter (I do have one other theory I'm working on), in which case you're probably not our dad after all and you can ignore all those bits. (But not the bit about the atlas.)

"I think you've pretty much covered everything," I said, reading over her shoulder. "But what's the other theory? Who else do you think it could be?"

Bauble acted like she hadn't heard. "You don't think he'll mind about the satsuma do you? I *would* have eaten it but I was worried about mycotoxins."

Myco-what-now? She looked so serious—like my opinion really mattered—that I felt doubly bad for not telling her the truth. I hoped this new theory of hers was better than the old one because there was no way this imaginary kitchen-kisser could be either one of our dads. Hers was well and truly dead—no chance of imagining that away again now I knew the full story— and mine had disappeared eleven years ago. So I did what any guilty big brother would do, and tickled her under the arms until she screamed for mercy. And then boofed her on the head with my pillow.

That's what woke Mum up, I think. The giggly screaming. She went straight from fast asleep to full-on fluster mode in the time it took her to get from her duvet to my bedroom.

"Why-didn't-anyone-wake-me-have-you-seen-what-the-time-is?" she gabbled, jabbing her finger at my numberless Batman wall clock like a mad woman. According to that it was bat sign past Commissioner Gordon. Also known as half-past ten.

"Don't take any notice of that," I told her. "It stopped working last week." Right before the whole mum-meltdown episode in the study, as it happened, but I decided not to mention that bit.

Bauble hid the Father Christmas letter behind her back as Mum made a lunge for her watch. "Twenty-past eight," she said quickly, beating her to it. "But it's alright. I've had my breakfast and I made my own lunch. With the right sandwiches and everything." *Not like the smelly tuna ones you gave me yesterday*—I bet that's what she was thinking, only she was too polite to say. "I thought you might need the extra sleep because I could hear you pacing round the house all night."

Mum's shoulders sagged and her face relaxed into a tired-looking smile. She leaned down and kissed the top of Bauble's head.

"I'm sorry if I kept you awake, sweetheart. But well done for getting everything ready on your own. You're a star. How did I get to have such a thoughtful grown-up girl?"

Probably because Dad was grown-up and thoughtful too. Unlike wild Finn the runaway. I guessed that meant there was no hope for me. But then Mum planted a big kiss on my head too. "With such a grown-up, understanding big brother," she added. "I must be the luckiest mum ever. Will you be alright here with Uncle Mike while I run Bauble to school? I'll ask him to pop over so there's someone in the house if you need him."

"I'll be fine," I told her, wishing she'd hurry up and go. *Whatever you do don't look at my bed.* I'd forgotten the stolen newspaper clipping about the zombie games designer hidden under my pillow. Only it wasn't hidden anymore, because my pillow was lying on the floor next to Bauble's feet. "Though I could really do with a drink of water," I added, hoping she'd take the hint.

It worked. As soon as she was gone, I tucked the newspaper cutting inside an old football annual instead (much safer!) and got back into bed. I had a lot to think about—like how to find a runaway father—and bed seemed like the best place to do it.

15

SANTA BABY

Mum made me pancakes for breakfast when she got home, with chocolate spread and raisins and half a can of squirty cream. *Mmm, squirty cream.* Anyone would think it was my birthday already but I guess she was just worried about me. About the effect of finding out the truth after all this time. *Surprise! We didn't know what present to get you this year so we've gone for a new dad! I hope you like him. Not that he likes you...*

I felt surprisingly alright though, considering. Cheerful even. Perhaps that's because it hadn't sunk in properly yet. Or perhaps it was because deep down I'd always known Dad wasn't coming back. That all the stuff about him being an undercover agent or a secret policeman was nothing more than wishful thinking. None of that had changed: he *still* wasn't coming back. But now? Now I had another dad who might.

"Do you have any photos of him?" I asked Mum as she finished drying up the breakfast dishes. Uncle Mike had gone straight home to finish off a translation so it had just been the two us. We'd spent the whole meal talking about everything *but* dads and family secrets. As if the events of last night had all been a dream. Or rather Mum talked, because she was in full-on chatter mode, and I nodded and mm-hmmed and nibbled runaway raisins out of my lap.

She talked about Bauble's new teacher, Miss Kershaw, who'd painted a life-size lion in the classroom window. About whether or not Rudy needed a new flea collar (judging by the amount of scratching going on under the table I'd guess the answer was probably 'yes'). About how she'd spotted four cats sniffing round the back of the Uncle Mikes' car on her way out that morning… and she *still* didn't show any signs of stopping. She was just starting off on some new story about pictures for a calendar when I cut in with my photo request.

"Don't worry if it's too upsetting," I added, "but..." *But I want to see if he looks like me.*

Mum paused, mid-plate-dry. "I'll see what I can do," she said. She wasn't exactly smiling, but she didn't seem too upset either. That was a good sign. "I'll need that key back—the one you took off my keyring last night."

Oops. I'd forgotten about that. Mum clearly hadn't though. This must be the bit where she finished with the fussing and the force-feeding and started with the telling off instead. I guessed not even a trip to hospital could save me from that.

"I'm sorry," I said, jumping in quickly before she could say anything else. Always good to get your apology in early. "For borrowing it without asking, I mean." See what I did there? Not *sorry for creeping round the house like a thief and stealing it from under your nose.* Or *sorry for going through your stuff.* At times like this you've got to pick your words carefully. Especially if you're secretly hoping for more information about your real dad. Like a full name and address.

I really did feel bad about the whole thief-creeping stuff. And about betraying Mum's trust. But I wasn't sorry it had happened. If I could have found out the truth without concussing myself that would have been even better, but it was a small price to pay for finding a whole new parent. And whatever was coming next— a big lecture, no more pocket money for the rest of the month, or an entire year's screen time ban—I still wouldn't have any regrets. But it never came. No punishment. No guilt trip. No nothing. She just nodded, like it was all water under a duck's back. No wait, I mean *off* a duck's back. Or is it water under the bridge? I don't know, but whatever Mum's water was doing it seemed to have forgiven me. "That's okay," she said, wrapping her arms round me and stroking the back of my head. "As long as *we're* okay now?"

"Yes," I said, hugging her back. "We're good." And I meant it.

We went upstairs to my bedroom together to fetch the key, which was still tucked away inside my trouser pocket with Mrs Whichey's family stick picture, and then Mum left me to get dressed.

"You'll feel better with some proper clothes on," she said, as if they were some kind of medicine: *take two pairs of pants three times a day before mealtimes.* I suppose it was more of a cunning plan to get me out of the way than anything else. Must have been, because let's face it, *nothing* feels better than pyjamas.

I did as I was told though and scrambled into some old jogging bottoms and a slightly whiffy Space Runner top from the washing basket. And then I hurried into Mum's bedroom to join her, hoping, *finally*, to see what was inside the famous black box.

There it was! Open at last. And it was full of... wait for it... no, not sparkling jewels or snakes. Not laser pistols and alien helmets. Not even fake passports and false moustaches. It was full of sheets of A4 paper and brown envelopes. And even though I knew that's what 'family documents' probably looked like—that's pretty much what all documents look like—it was still disappointing after such a long build-up.

Mum pulled out an envelope—not a brown one as it turned out, this one was white with 'NOEL' written across the middle—and handed it to me. Almost. She hovered it above my outstretched hands for a while and then pulled it back into her chest.

"What's that?" I asked.

"A letter."

Really? You don't say.

"A letter your dad wrote for you when you were little."

Wow! I thought. There I was planning to write to

him—to find out if he'd changed his mind about having a son—and he'd beaten me to it!

"When he first found out he was ill," added Mum.

Oh. Not that dad then, I thought with a flash of disappointment. And then I felt bad for being disappointed, as if I'd already replaced him. *Sorry Dad.*

"He wanted me to give it to you when you were older," she said, dabbing at her eyes with the back of her thumb as she clung to the letter. "Old enough to understand."

I nodded, in what I hoped was an 'old enough' but pleased kind of way. Certainly not a disappointed nod, anyway.

"Can I see it? What does it say?"

"I don't know," said Mum. "I never saw the finished letter, only the photo he chose to go with it. I mean, we talked about it first obviously—about what he wanted to say—but it's very much a message from him to you." She stopped to blow her nose. "I can read it with you now, if you'd like. If you think you're ready. Or you can read it on your own if you'd rather. No pressure either way though. And we can just as easily put it back in the box for another time. I realise it's a lot to take in all at once."

"No," I said, without even stopping to think about it. About the effect it might have on me. "I want to read it. On my own, if that's okay." I didn't want to hurt her feelings but I didn't want her there reading over my shoulder, crying and making me feel bad.

"Of course," she said, a little too quickly. A little too brightly. "But I'll be right here if you need me."

Mum finally let go of the envelope and I carried it back to my bedroom, cradled in my hands like a scared baby bird. It was me who was the scared one though. Even though I knew it was only words inside (well, words and a photo), I sat staring at the envelope for a full five minutes before I plucked up enough courage to open it. They might be the most important words I'd ever read in my whole life. Quite possibly the most precious ones. And once I'd read them—whatever it was they said—there was no going back. I couldn't exactly *un*read them, could I?

I took a deep breath and eased out the folded sheet of cream notepaper inside, thinking about how Dad was the last person to touch it. Wow. That was weird. Really weird. I found myself stroking along the fold with my fingertip as if some little piece of him might still be lurking there. Some last memory imprinted into the paper for me to find. But it felt exactly like normal paper. It smelt like normal paper too—a bit musty maybe, after all that time shut up in a box—but no last trace of aftershave to hold on to. No special scent to trigger any long-buried memories.

Come on then, I told myself. *Let's get on with it...*

My Dearest Noel,

This is the hardest letter I've ever had to write— I'm on my tenth attempt already!

I'm trying my best to picture you as you are now, reading this—my precious little boy all grown up! Bet you don't like being called 'precious' or 'little' now! Sorry about that. Anyway, what I mean is it's even harder to write without knowing what you're like now. Do you still do that funny thing with your eyebrows when you're excited? Does your hair still curl into a perfect 'S' at the back of your neck? Do you still like mashed banana sandwiches? Are you still ticklish behind your knees?

I can only guess at these things, of course, but there's no doubt in my mind that you've grown into a fine young man. The kind of young man I'd be proud to call my son. That goes without saying, of course, because wherever life takes you I'll always be proud of you, Noel. And you'll always be my son, no matter what it says on your birth certificate.

You and your mum have brought more joy and meaning to my life than I ever thought possible. Thank you for letting me share your first years. Am I sad that we couldn't have had longer? That I couldn't still be there with you now, sharing new adventures with you? Yes, of course I am. I'd be lying if I pretended otherwise. I feel sad and angry and guilty for leaving you both. But above all, I feel grateful. Grateful and privileged to have spent this time together with you. To have known and loved you.

I guess this is the part of the letter where I'm supposed to pass on my worldly wisdom and expert advice. Follow your dreams… the only things you regret in life are those you didn't do… you know, that sort of thing… Only I'm not sure I'm quite wise enough myself to be dishing out advice to anyone else! Besides, I don't need a crystal ball to tell me you're going to turn out just fine. More than fine, in fact. A model young man, destined for success and happiness. Yes, I have total one hundred percent faith in you and

I know the rest of the world will love you as much as I do.

You probably don't remember me by now and that's fine. That's good! Your mum may well have met someone else by now and that's good too. That's the way it should be and I'm happy that she's happy. But even if you don't remember my silly jokes or my monkey impression (that always makes you laugh!), please don't ever forget how much you mean to me. How much I love you. How much I always will.

Be happy, Noel. Be loved. Look after your little brother or sister for me (we just found out yesterday!). And your mum of course. I know you will.

Forever and always,

Your loving Daddy xx

And that was it. My message from beyond the grave. Only it wasn't all spooky or weird, it was more... well, I don't know exactly. It's hard to explain *what* it was, or how it made me feel. Sort of happy and sad and lonely, but also loved, and lucky and cheated all at the same time. All mixed up in a tangled knot of feelings. Mum was right. It *was* a lot to take in at once. No wonder she'd kept the truth from me for so long.

And she was right about Dad too—he really *had* loved me.

I peeled the photograph away from the inside of the envelope with shaking hands, hoping to put a face to the words I'd just read. Only Mum had got that bit wrong—there were actually *two* photographs, not one. Maybe she'd forgotten after all this time. Or maybe Dad had slipped in an extra picture later as an afterthought. The top one was of baby me, cuddled in tight against his chest. I couldn't see his face very well though because he was looking down at me instead of the camera. In fact, I couldn't see anything very well suddenly because my eyes had gone all prickly and blurry. I wiped them on the cuff of my Space Runner top and moved on to the second picture.

I was older in this one—like a proper mini-person—and Dad was grinning straight out of the photograph, looking exactly as I remembered him. That's the funny thing: I hadn't remembered him at all up until then. If you'd asked me ten minutes earlier what he looked like I wouldn't have had a clue. But something clicked when I saw him, like someone had pressed a light switch in my head.

Dad! How could I have forgotten that smile, or the

tiny crinkles round his eyes? Or the dimple in his chin? He looked like… Wait, I knew *exactly* who he looked like… Bauble! Same chin. Same turned-up nose. Same clever-looking blue eyes. The only *real* differences were hairy ones: they both had straight blond hair but Bauble didn't have any stubble and Dad didn't have plaits. Apart from that, the family likeness was unmissable. Maybe that's why Mum hadn't wanted any photos round the house. I clearly didn't get my brown eyes, smooth chin and dark crazy hair from her, and it wouldn't take a genius (or a Bauble brain) to figure out I didn't get them from Dad either.

Of course Bauble might not even notice how little like Dad I looked if *she* saw the photo. Not at first, anyway. She'd be too busy looking at the hats Dad and I were wearing to think about the shape of our chins. The matching red Santa hats.

16

STICK MAN

"Can I come in?" said Mum, from the doorway.

I nodded but didn't look up. I was too busy staring at the photos, trying to keep up with the crazy thoughts flitting through my head. Could it have been a ghost Bauble saw in the kitchen with Mum? Had Dad come back to see her wearing the exact same Santa hat, to remind her of happier times? Could you kiss a ghost, though, that was the question? Or would your lips come out through the back of their head? *Yuck.* And could ghosts draw cartoon birds and write messages? I mean I knew it was an 'F' on that robin postcard, not an 'N', but maybe that was short for a nickname only he and Mum knew. Or 'F' for Finn? No. It couldn't be from him. I'd have noticed it before now if she'd held on to it all those years, sitting right there on her desk in full view of anyone who wandered in. Admittedly the letters were more sloped and curly than Dad's, but maybe death did funny things to people's handwriting. Just like it did funny things to their choice of summer hats…

Mum sat down beside me on the bed and pointed at the second photograph.

"I remember the day I took that," she said. "In the grotto on the top floor of Harpers & Plym. We all dressed up specially for the occasion—Santa hats all round—but you screamed when it got to your turn, and we had to rush you out the shop without getting your present." She laughed at the memory. "I think it was the big white beard that set you off. Or the sinister-looking nodding reindeer in the background. But this was taken on the way in, while you were still waiting in the queue. You enjoyed that bit!"

I looked at her eyes. She was doing an excellent job of not crying. There we were talking about Dad and she was still smiling! Perhaps she'd used up all her tears the night before.

"Mum, can I ask you something?"

"Of course," she said, keeping her voice all bright and chirpy like she wasn't at all worried what the question might be.

"Do you believe in ghosts?" I asked. *Was that Dad Bauble saw you kissing in the kitchen?*

"What?" She clearly hadn't been expecting that. She took a deep breath in as if the answer needed extra oxygen. "No, sweetheart. I don't. But I don't believe death is the end either. I think people live on in the hearts of everyone who loved them."

Even my real dad, Finn? She must have loved him too once upon a time.

Mum reached out and put her hand on my chest—right over the Space Runner logo. "In their hearts," she said again, "and in their memories."

"What about in their kitchens?"

"*Kitchens?*" she echoed, a mixture of laughter and surprise in her voice. "You are silly, Noel."

So much for that theory.

"Look." She pulled me towards her, my head pressing against the bony bit of her shoulder. It wasn't very comfy to be honest, but I didn't want to upset her by pulling away. Especially not if I wanted to ask her about Finn. "Nothing will ever change what you felt for each other. And anytime you want to talk about him—about anything—I'm here for you. You know that, don't you?"

"Yes." I told her. "In fact, I *do* have another question…"

"About Dad?"

"Kind of." I felt bad even mentioning Finn with Dad's letter still there in my lap. With that photo of the two of us staring up at me. But I kept thinking how much Dad looked like Bauble—how he wasn't just in her heart or her memory, he was *part* of her—and realised I still wanted to know where *I'd* come from. Who *I* looked like. Even with all the mixed up emotions I'd felt reading Dad's words, that hadn't changed. It was tricky though. I didn't want to hurt Mum's feelings, which is why I went for a little white lie instead.

"We've been doing a family tree thing at school," I said, laying everything down on my bedside table and rescuing the bedraggled-looking stick picture from my school trousers. I flattened it out as best as I could and waved it under Mum's nose. "And Mrs Whichey said it would be really good if we could add some photos." What she'd really said was, *leave your finished trees on my desk and clear up ready for home time.* Which was *almost* the same thing. Easy mistake to make.

"Oh," said Mum, frowning at my less than impressive artistic efforts. "We seem to have a lot of red sausages in our family. Including two particularly curly ones called Frank and Felicity. And what's that? A squirrel?"

"They're not sausages," I explained. "They're bananas." Like that made so much more sense. "To be honest I got a bit bored while everyone else was putting in all their aunts and uncles and cousins. A bit carried away with the red pen. That's why I need some photos, you see. To cover up the sausages. I mean bananas."

Mum didn't look convinced. Or maybe she was worried how I was going to fit two different dads on the same leaf.

"I guess I *could* scan in the Santa hat photo and print you out a smaller copy," she agreed. But she didn't say anything about Finn. Perhaps she was hoping I'd forget about him now I'd read Dad's letter. Perhaps she was still mad at him for running away and didn't think he deserved a place on my fruity family stick. Or maybe he'd been hideously ugly, with a hairy pig nose, enormous eyebrows and giant elephant ears, and she didn't want me worrying I might turn out the same.

"What about my other dad?" I blurted out, before I had a chance to change my mind. "Is there a photo of him I could have?"

Mum shut her eyes for a moment and squeezed her lips together. She was about to say something—I know she was—only she was saved by the bell. The doorbell.

17

DID YOU HEAR THE ONE ABOUT THE CUSTARD CREAMS?

"Oh heck," Mum muttered, checking her watch and jumping up off the bed like she'd been stung. I don't know what by exactly, a giant bottom wasp or something. And then she went zooming off down the stairs at top speed, like some kind of Mum-Road-Runner. *I* get told off for racing on the stairs. 'The only place you'll be going in a hurry is hospital,' that's what she always says. But Mum had clearly managed it without a second trip to A&E because I could hear her opening the front door.

"Goodness me! Hello!" she said, sounding like she might fall over with sheer surprise. You know that TV show, 'Everyone's a Winner', where Brian Big Bucks (I'm guessing that's not his real name) rocks up on someone's doorstep with an enormous cardboard cheque? And the lucky winner starts squealing, *Oh my goodness, I don't believe it,* about a hundred times? That's what Mum sounded like. Not quite so squealy, but the exact same level of amazed disbelief. I went running down the stairs after her to see who it was.

"Walk!" she shouted up at me. "I don't want another trip to hospital, thank you very much. Noel took a bit of a tumble yesterday," she said, turning back to whoever it was at the door. Was that the sort of information you shared with Brian and an army of TV cameras? Probably not. "He's fine," she went on, "but I'm keeping him off school for a couple of days to make sure."

"Ah," said a familiar man's voice. *Definitely* not Brian Big Bucks. It wasn't nearly posh enough. "I see. Poor thing. How are you feeling now, Noel?"

I reached the bottom of the stairs and peered past Mum. Of course! It was Mr Marsh. For a moment, I thought he might have come to check if we'd been practising or not. And then I remembered we'd only just had our lesson the day before. It felt more like weeks with everything that had happened.

"Not too bad, thank you," I said, joining Mum in the doorway. "I did have another go at the Beethoven tune before I hit my head."

Mr Marsh beamed. "Excellent. I wish all my pupils were as keen as that." And then his face fell. "You didn't hit it *on* the piano, did you?"

"No, nothing like that," said Mum quickly. "A nasty tumble, that's all. Mr Marsh was just dropping off my bracelet," she explained, ruffling my hair. "It must have flown off yesterday when I was clapping."

"Yes, that's right. It must have done," agreed Mr Marsh.

"Would you like to come in for a cuppa now you're here?" said Mum. "I was about to put the kettle on."

No you weren't, I thought. *You were about to look for a photo of my real dad.*

"I don't know…" Mr Marsh looked super serious, as if it was the trickiest decision he'd ever had to make. Grown-ups are a bit weird like that sometimes. It seemed like a simple enough question to me. *Do you want a cup of tea? Yes or no?*

"Go on then," he said at last. "If you're sure I'm not disturbing you."

Yes, you are actually. You're disturbing some pretty serious Dad-stuff as it happens.

"Not at all," Mum assured him. "I might even open some custard creams if you play your cards right."

"Ha ha ha ha ha," they both laughed, as if 'custard creams' was the funniest joke ever. Not like snotolatc digestives. That really *would* have been a good one. Garry Baldy biscuits, even. But custard creams? You can't do *anything* funny with them. Like I said, grownups are weird.

The doorbell rang again about ten minutes later. Mum had been so busy giving Mr Marsh a blow-by-blow account of our visit to the hospital (apart from the Dad stuff—she skipped over those bits) that she hadn't even filled the kettle yet. Tea and comedy custard creams still seemed like a distant dream.

"I don't know who that can be," she said, looking puzzled, as if her superhero X-ray vision had suddenly stopped working. *No, it's no good. I can't see through solid wooden doors today for some reason.*

"Sorry," she told Mr Marsh. "I'd better go and see. Put the kettle on for me, Noel, there's a good boy."

It still wasn't Brian Big Bucks with a giant cardboard cheque. Shame. It was Uncle Mike—Big Mike, I mean—with a bag of frozen fish pie filling. Only it wasn't frozen at all anymore, judging by the smell following him down the hallway.

"Oh hello," he said to Mr Marsh. "Fred, isn't it?

157

Sorry, Stella, I didn't realise you had company. I just popped round to see how the patient was doing, and to return this." He waved the stinky fish bag in front of Mum's face as she followed him into the kitchen. "It was still in the car from last night—no wonder we've had half the neighbourhood cats scratching over the paintwork."

"Good to see you again," said Mr Marsh, as if he and Uncle Mike were old friends. Which they couldn't have been, because otherwise Mike would've known his name was Showpan, not Fred. But I guess Mr Marsh was too polite to say anything. Just like he was too polite to gag at the disgusting fishy fumes wafting under his nose.

Mum, on the other hand, looked like she was about to be sick. "Noel," she said. "Take that bag outside and put it in the black bin for me. It's stinking the whole house out."

Put the kettle on, Noel. Take the fish out, Noel. Forget about finding that photograph you wanted, Noel.

"Thank you," she whispered, as if she'd read my mind. "Sorry we didn't get to finish our talk, sweetheart—it would have been rude not to invite them in. I haven't forgotten though."

By the time I got back from my seafood disposal mission, the others were deep in conversation. Mr Marsh was telling Uncle Mike about some programme he'd seen on telly where fish started falling out the sky. This weird weather thing sucked them up out of a nearby pond and then rained them back down again in someone's garden. It sounded pretty cool actually.

"There you are," said Mum when she saw me, as if I'd been gone for hours. "Mr Marsh was just telling me how he and Uncle Mike met."

"At the aquarium?" I asked. It seemed like a sensible enough guess to me, given that everyone kept talking about fish.

"No. At a concert," she said. "That's right, isn't it? A classical music concert."

"Oh." I was more interested in the fish. "What about when they landed? Were they dead?"

"We had a mini concert of our own yesterday, didn't we Noel?" said Mum, speaking right over the top of me. "Bauble was still talking about it on the way to school this morning," she told Mr Marsh. "She said she wants to be a pianist when she grows up now, as well as a brain surgeon."

Mr Marsh looked ridiculously pleased, like she'd just offered him a million pounds. "I always wanted to be a footballer," he said, "much to my mum and dad's disappointment. Only it turned out I was better at playing music than matches. Still am, sadly, even though in my head I'm the next Petro Ollander!" Everyone laughed. "And to answer your question about the fish, Noel, I'm afraid I don't know. Though I doubt they were feeling too *brill* afterwards. Even if they didn't end up as fish pie mix they probably had terrible *haddocks*."

Ha ha! Haddocks… Headaches. That was a good one. Brill was a kind of fish too, wasn't it? I seemed to remember Bauble reading out something about them when she got that animal encyclopaedia out the school library. It was supposed to be 'Reference Only', but she'd read all the non-reference ones so they let her borrow it anyway.

"I think I'd feel a bit *eel* if I'd been sucked into the sky like that," added Mr Marsh, pulling a fishy face. "Maybe a bit *crabby* too!"

For some reason, I always used to think of piano teachers as old ladies. Little old ladies with grey hair buns, like Great Granny Gum-Gums in *Mutant*

Monkey Man. But Mr Marsh couldn't have been less like an old lady if he tried. Bauble was right—he was cool! He'd passed the no-meat-clothing test with flying colours (thank goodness—I was still haunted by that image of Mrs Manzo and her sausages) and now it turned out he liked football as well. Petro Ollander had been my favourite player ever since he scored that hat trick against Arsenal.

Mr Marsh even told proper funny stories, like the one about his dad and the stray dog in the airing cupboard. And the one about the runaway go-kart they made together, that crashed into next door's greenhouse. In fact, most of his stories were about his dad. He smiled every time he mentioned him like they were still best friends even though he was grown up now.

I'd always dreamt that's what having a dad would be like. Football in the park, silly family games, building contraptions in the garage… Dad and I never had a chance to do all those things. No matter how much he'd loved me like his own son, it didn't change the fact that he'd gone. But maybe there was still a chance with Finn. Maybe we could turn back the clock and start again.

18

GENIUS GENES

Mr Marsh and Uncle Mike ended up staying for lunch, which meant I didn't get to finish my Finn chat with Mum. But that was okay. I was too busy enjoying myself to think about it that much, anyway. But then, after Mr Marsh finally left, something happened which changed all that. The kind of something that meant I couldn't *stop* thinking about my real dad, even if I tried.

I was coming back from the toilet when I overheard Mum and Uncle Mike talking. I don't know why, but something made me stop and listen. Yes, I know what you're thinking—unless you're still trying to come up with a funny custard cream joke, that is, in which case good luck, you'll need it. You're thinking that, unless you happen to be James Bond, it's not very nice to eavesdrop. I agree, it's not very nice at all. But then neither is going through your mum's private stuff or stealing her keys. A little bit of skulking in the hallway with my ear pressed against the kitchen door didn't seem too bad compared to that. And it *was* all in a good cause. All part of my latest father-finding mission.

"I was worried Noel might have guessed," Mum was saying. "Because I'm pretty sure he saw that postcard. It doesn't look like he's put two and two together yet, though. And it *was* only signed 'F', luckily. That could be anyone."

I held my breath. The postcard from 'F'? Did that mean 'F' was someone I knew?

Finn! Yes! I must have been right the first time. Who else could it be?

"Would it be such a bad thing if he did?" said Uncle Mike. "If everything was out in the open?"

So Mum *had* kept it all this time. But what did Uncle Mike mean about 'everything' being out in the open? That sounded like a much bigger secret than an old postcard. Unless it wasn't an *old* postcard at all? *Holey Tinsel Trousers!* Was it Finn Bauble saw in the Santa hat? Had he finally come back for Mum after all these years?

Mum didn't answer straight away. It sounded like she was thinking.

"I don't know, Mike. Noel's got enough on his plate right now. He's still getting his head round all this stuff about Nick, without complicating things even more. Besides, it's still early days and we don't want to say anything to the kids until we're sure."

Mum and Finn! My real dad! How amazing would that be? I rubbed my nose, trying to get rid of a tickle inside my nostrils before it turned into a full-blown sneeze. It must have been the lavender-scented cleaner Mum uses on the doors. That often sets me off.

"Whatever you think's best," said Uncle Mike. "You've got my blessing anyway, for what it's worth."

"Thanks, Mike," said Mum. "That means a lot. And who knows, perhaps if we're still together at Christmas…"

Still together?! It was true then! Only I never got to find out what would happen at Christmas—a special announcement? A party, to celebrate?—because that sneeze was refusing to go away. I bet that never happens to James Bond. Not unless he goes on a really dusty spying mission. Or battles baddies in a pepper factory.

Ah-ah-ah-ah-ah-a-choooooo! A big wet splatty one it was, too, followed by a pair of little diddlers, for luck: *Achoo, achoo.* That was it. By the time I'd finished sneezing, the subject had been well and truly changed, marking the end of my eavesdropping efforts. But that was okay. I'd heard all I needed to.

I was bursting to tell Bauble about Finn, when we went to collect her from school on the way to the supermarket. I'd been thinking about it all the way there, about how perfect life would be after Christmas. All four of us together like a proper family. But I couldn't say anything. Not with Mum sitting in the front seat, listening in. Bauble didn't even know Finn existed yet, let alone that he and Mum were dating again. I had to settle for telling her about Mr Marsh's visit instead. She was dead jealous when she heard he'd stayed for lunch—for tuna sandwiches and paprika crisps.

"I wish I'd been there," she said. "It's not fair."

"You'd have had to miss school," I pointed out, knowing she couldn't argue with that. It would take more than an inspiring piano teacher to drag Miss Super-Brains away from lessons. "Besides, you don't even like tuna."

"I could have had cheese spread," she said, looking sulky. "And school was rubbish anyway. Our class is doing that stupid 'What Makes Me Me' project on families as well now, and Chloe Corston kept going on about her cousins in America and how amazing her grandma's cooking is. It was *so* boring. And then Ben Matterson said that families needed a mum *and* a dad and Miss Kershaw thought I was crying, even though I just had a runny nose and my eyes were watering."

"Ben Matterson's an idiot," I said, trying to make her feel better. Even though I wanted a mum *and* a dad too. But Bauble carried on as if she hadn't heard, explaining how even though she definitely, *definitely* hadn't been crying, Miss Kershaw had given her permission to swap the family tree project for something else instead.

"So I'm doing mine on genes," she said, glancing up at Mum in the rear view mirror.

I was waiting for her to tell us about humans and fruit flies again, but she never did. She said she was going to investigate how genes got passed down through families. The ones that decided what colour eyes children had and whether they had chin-dimples or not. That sort of thing.

Mum's knuckles went white as her hands tightened round the steering wheel.

"Maybe you could research the Royal Family instead?" she suggested.

Bauble wasn't having any of it though. "No, this is much more interesting. Can we stop off at the library on the way and get some books out?"

"You're lucky," I told her. "We had to do the family tree thing in class. *And* we need to find photos to put on it." Lie, lie. Hint, hint. I couldn't exactly ask Mum about the picture of Finn now—not with Bauble there—but I didn't want her to think I'd forgotten about it. I wanted to see what he looked like more than ever now. "*You* know," I said, raising my voice even louder. "Photos of our family."

Mum didn't say anything although I'm pretty sure she heard. And then Bauble was off talking about Mr Marsh again, asking me whether he'd done any more snowman pictures and quizzing Mum about the lost bracelet.

I thought Mum would be happy to change the subject, but her knuckles didn't get any less white, and I'm pretty sure the pulse in her neck was going as well.

Perhaps she was nervous about Bauble looking into our family genes. About what she might find. Or maybe she was fed up with me going on about photos all the time.

She barely said a word when we stopped at the library. And she was quiet all the way round the supermarket too, even when we bumped into the school lollipop lady in the bakery aisle. They chat for hours normally, snarling up the traffic while they have a natter in the middle of the road.

"Speaking of cakes," said the lollipop lady, "I got to have a sneaky peek at June last night." At least I think that's what she said. I was still thinking about the story she'd been telling us. About how her dog's vomit turned bright pink after he ate an entire plate of red velvet cupcakes. And then I started wondering what colour it would be if he'd eaten a Battenburg instead. Yellow or pink? Or a sort of peachy mixture of the two?

The lollipop lady let out a whistle. "Wow," she said. "The way she got those cream cakes to balance on her bikini top like that... Such a good photo."

Woah. Hang on a minute. Not *another* weirdo decorating their swimwear with random bits of food?

What was wrong with everyone? First Mrs Manzo, then the mysterious Mr March. And now this June woman. Not to mention the grapey greengrocer photo I'd spotted the night before. I pulled a *yuck-I-might-be-sick* face at Bauble, but she was busy trying to read the list of ingredients on a box of Bakewell tarts. In Spanish.

"Definitely one for the kitchen wall," said the lollipop lady.

Ugh. No wonder her dog had been sick if he had to look at photos like that all the time. I bet it was nothing to do with red velvet cupcakes.

19

I'M DREAMING OF A FIGHT CHRISTMAS

I've got it! A brand new biscuit pun: Pus-turd Creams!
I must remember to tell Bauble that next time Mum
offers us some. Anyway, where was I? Oh yes, in the
bakery aisle with the lollipop lady and her vomity dog
story. That was as action-packed as the evening got.
We helped Mum unpack the shopping, had dinner
(macaroni cheese), and then we all watched some lame
game show together until I fell asleep on the sofa. It
must've been all the sleepless excitement of the night
before catching up with me.

Mum checked my temperature and then packed me
off to bed, even though it was still early. And, just this
once, I decided not to argue. Not that I was planning
on going back to sleep. Not yet. I wanted to reply to
Dad's letter while it was nice and quiet. I know that

sounds crazy but it felt like I still had things to say to him, especially after listening in on Mum's conversation. Plus I wanted to plan out some fun father and son things to do with Finn after Christmas—once it was all official. So I got into my pyjamas and brushed my teeth, then tiptoed into Bauble's room to get the special investigation notebook. She'd shown me exactly where to find it, tucked away in the hollow space behind her under-bed drawers. It was only hidden from Mum, not me.

I was relieved to see she hadn't added anything else to her EVIDENCE FOR DAD BEING FATHER CHRISTMAS list. Maybe she'd finally realised how bonkers it all was. Even so, the sooner Bauble knew the full truth, the better. Not that I understood it *all* yet—like what Finn was doing in trunks and a Santa hat in August—but it felt mean keeping her in the dark. Even if she was upset at first, like I was, she had a right to know what was going on.

I turned over more pages, looking for a blank sheet, and found a brand new list instead. Perhaps it was something to do with her secret back-up theory—the one she'd mentioned in her letter to Santa. But there was no neatly underlined title on this one, just a random collection of questions and words:

Why F? Why not S?
snowman
wishful thinking?
photograph on the wall
laughing

Huh? That made about as much sense as the time she told me about some special Italian cheese with live maggots in it. Why would anyone want to eat that? Or the time she tried explaining algebra sums to me halfway through an episode of *The Simpsons*. Still, it hardly mattered now. The investigation was officially over.

The next page was blank so I got into bed, picked up my stick of rock pen, and started my letter to Dad. Yes, I knew perfectly well he wouldn't be able to read it. I wasn't planning on addressing it to heaven and sticking a stamp on it, or anything. But there was stuff I needed to say—stuff I needed to get out—and that was the only way I could think of doing it.

I thought it would be hard. I thought I'd struggle to find the right words. But they seemed to flow out the end of my pen all on their own.

Dear Dad, I wrote (you could probably have guessed that bit),

Mum gave me your letter. The one you wrote before you—well, you know. I just wanted to say thank you as well, for looking after me when I was little. For everything you said about loving me. I still love you too, even if I can't remember much about our time together. I wish we could have had longer. I wish you were still here now.

You said it was OK if Mum met someone else. That you wanted her to be happy. I hope you meant it because she has. It's Finn, my birth dad. I haven't met him yet but I do want to. At least, I think I do (if that's alright with you). As long as he doesn't run away again and upset her. He'll never replace you, but it would be nice to have someone else apart from the Uncle Mikes to act out Space Runner fights with. And play football in the park. You know, dad stuff.

It doesn't mean I don't love you anymore though. You'll still be my dad, even if you're in heaven now. At least I got to meet you. Not like Bauble. She's really clever, by the way. Does she get that from you? I'm

not. I'm just normal. Though I think I might be quite good at the piano. It's a bit hard to tell as I've only had one lesson so far.

I forgot to say, Bauble looks just like you too. Only without the stubble. I promise I'll look after her for you. And Mum.

Lots of love,

Noel xxx

P.S. I'm quite good at snot and biscuit jokes too. Like Snotolate Digestives and Gary Baldies.

I felt so much better for putting it all down on paper. Like some of the jumbled up thoughts in my head were lying down in neater rows now. I folded it up with the one he'd written me, and tucked them inside the old football annual next to the newspaper picture of Mr Zombie-Zapper Okenson. That was the last thing I remember. Seriously. I don't even remember getting back into bed. One minute, I was there at the bookcase holding the annual and the next thing I knew I was knee deep in a weird dream about my dads. Both of them this time…

In the red corner was Dad Number One, Nick, dressed in the same cape he'd been wearing last time.

When he was out in the garden, waving keys at me through the glass. He seemed to have lost the meat eye mask somewhere along the way though. Perhaps he'd cooked and eaten it between dreams. And in the blue corner was Finn (also known as Dad Number Two), sporting a dark turquoise cape and stick-on elf ears with pointy tips. Don't ask me how my brain dreamt *those* up. Apart from the ears, his head was completely bare. Seriously. No hat. No hair. Balder than a Gary Baldy biscuit he was. Shinier than our shiny-headed headmaster. And as for his face… well, it looked pretty much exactly like my face, only without the chickenpox scar.

If you're thinking all this sounds like the warm-up to a wrestling match you're spot on. That's *exactly* what it was like. Only they weren't fighting for a trophy, or glory, they were fighting for me.

"He's *my* son," cricd Dad, hurtling towards Finn, his right arm spinning like a windmill. "And he always will be. You had your chance and you blew it."

"Correction," yelled Finn, dodging out of the way with some dainty ballerina-style footwork. "I think you'll find he's *my* son. You had *your* chance and *you* blew it. My turn now."

"I died, you idiotic waste of space," said Dad. "I didn't run away like a coward..." He ducked as Finn launched a high kick towards his head. It was a bit like the fight scene at the end of *Space Runner III* now I come to think about it. A *lot* like it. There were even some of those funny orange alien things in the front row, cheering them on: *Da-ad, Da-ad, Da-ad*. I'm not sure they really knew what side they were on, they were just enjoying the show. I'm not sure *I* knew what side I was on either. Perhaps I wanted them both to win.

"If you let him down again I'll pummel you to a paste," roared Dad, charging, head down like a bull, towards Finn's stomach. There's a lot of talk about paste-pummelling in the *Space Runner* films.

Finn leapfrogged right over Dad at the last minute. "I'll never let him down again," he shouted back. "There's not a day goes by when I don't think about him. When I don't wish I'd stayed. I'm going to make up for it now though. I'm going to be the best dad *ever!*"

The aliens in the front row cheered and clapped their hands. "Not just to Noel," he went on, "but to Bauble too. *And* I'm going to marry Stella so we can be a proper family."

"You'd better not mess them around!" Dad did a weird karate chop thing in mid-air. "Otherwise…"

Otherwise what? I never got to find out because suddenly the Death Bomber from *Space Runner II* came hurtling out of the sky, crushing down on my chest like a… like… well, like an enormous space ship really. Only this particular Death Bomber turned out to be a soft squidgy dressing-gowned one, with minty toothpaste breath.

"Oh Noel," came Bauble's quivery voice as she jolted me awake. "Mum just told me."

"Wharrrr?" I opened one eye to see her pale face looming above mine. What about the others? Where had they gone?

"She told me about your real dad," whispered Bauble. "The one who ran away."

No! He's come back, I wanted to tell her. *He's going to marry Mum so we can be a proper family.* I almost said it out loud until I realised the last bit was only a dream. No orange aliens. No caped crusader fathers fighting over me.

"That's why we look so different," Bauble said. "Because we're only half-related. Which means I'm only half your sister now. And you're only half my brother." She looked like she was about to cry.

I forced myself to wake up properly, sitting up and wrapping my arms around her. "And what do you get if you add two halves together, Super Brain?"

"A whole," she said.

"Exactly. We're a team, you and me. Always have been. Always will. Who cares if we've got the same colour eyes or not?"

Bauble nodded, her head bobbing up and down against my chest.

"What else did Mum tell you about him?" I asked. "About Finn?" *Full name? Favourite football player? Level of baldness? What he was doing with a Santa hat in the middle of summer?*

"Nothing, really," said Bauble. "Only that she had to tell me what was happening because it wasn't fair asking you to keep it secret. That it was better to get it all out in the open. She said it won't change anything though."

"It won't," I promised her. *Not unless it changes things for the better.* "Did she say if she'd heard from him lately? Whether he'd sent her any postcards…?"

"No," said Bauble. "But she gave me a letter from Dad that he wrote after they found out I was on the way."

"Me too," I told her. "What does yours say?"

"I haven't read it yet. I don't know if I want to. Because then he's really dead, isn't he?"

"Not Santa Claus, you mean?"

She nodded again, reaching into her dressing gown pocket, as tears began rolling down her cheeks. "It was a stupid idea, anyway." She pulled out the letter to Father Christmas she'd shown me that morning and ripped it into little pieces.

"Hey! Don't cry. It's going to be okay. You can share *my* dad," I told her. "I'm pretty sure he's the 'F' who wrote that postcard to Mum. I heard her talking to Uncle Mike about it today. And it was probably *him* you saw kissing her under the wishing bow. Anyone could have made the same mistake."

Bauble picked up the Investigation Notebook from my bedside table (I'd forgotten I was supposed to be keeping it hidden), and turned to the new list I'd been looking at earlier. The one with all the random words:

Why F? Why not S?

snowman

wishful thinking?

photograph on the wall

laughing

She sniffed, wiping her nose on the cuff of her dressing gown. "Are you *sure* it was an 'F'? Not an 'S'?"

"One hundred percent. 'F' for Finn. Why? Who's 'S'? And what's with the photograph on the wall? Not Mrs Manzo again?"

Bauble shrugged her shoulders. "I don't know, perhaps I'm wrong. Just like I was wrong about the whole Father Christmas thing. But I don't think you should get your hopes up about your birth dad. It definitely wasn't him in the kitchen, I know that much."

"How?" I snapped, a sudden burst of anger flaring up in my chest. "How do you know? Have you ever met him?" *I* didn't even know what he looked like, so what made her such an expert all of a sudden?

Either Bauble didn't notice the new crossness in my voice, or she didn't care. "Look, he hasn't been bothered about finding you or Mum before now," she went on, like she was the big sister and I was the little brother who didn't know anything. "And I mean statistically speaking..."

Statistics! This wasn't about maths and numbers. This was my dad we were talking about. My chance to be part of a normal family for once.

"Shut up!" I said. "You're just jealous 'cause I've

still got a dad and you haven't."

I hadn't meant to say it. I don't even know where the words came from. But there they were, tumbling out of my mouth in a horrible spiteful snarl that sent Bauble reeling backwards in shock. I was shocked too. We never argue. Not properly, I mean.

"I was right about something," she said, as a fresh stream of teary snot escaped out of her left nostril. "You *are* only half my brother now. The nasty half." And with that she went rushing out the room, taking the Investigation Notebook with her.

Wait, I should have called after her. *I'm sorry, I didn't mean it.* I should have followed her, told her what Mum had said about her new relationship. Made her understand. But I didn't. Wherever the sudden burst of anger had come from, it wasn't in a hurry to go back again. I lay in bed, fuming, waiting for her to come and apologise to me instead. Only she didn't.

"It *was* him," I muttered at the empty room, trying to push away the sneaking doubts she'd planted in my mind. "You'll see."

20

MY OTHER DAD, THE LIVING LEGEND

Two weird dad dreams in one night! That had to be a record. Perhaps it was Mum's macaroni cheese that did it. Isn't there something about too much cheese late at night giving you nightmares? Not that these were bad dreams. In fact, if you took out all the gruesome kissy-kissy-snog stuff, the second one was pretty good really:

It was exactly like Bauble had described it—Mum and a man in a Santa hat underneath the wishing bow. No orange aliens watching this time though. Just me, spying through the banisters.

"Oh Stella," said the man. "I've missed you and Noel so much. Seeing you again—it's like my Christmas came early this year."

"Oh Finn," said Mum, twisting a bit of tinsel round

her wrist like a bracelet. "We've missed you too."

Santa-Finn took her in his arms. *Yuck.* "I swear I'm going to make it up to you." Kiss, kiss. *Yuck, yuck, yuck.* "And I'll never leave you again…"

When I woke up, it was morning. And there was a new pile of photographs waiting for me on the bedside table, as if by magic. Not of Dad this time, but Finn: two of him on his own, one of a very young Mum and him making lovey-dovey goo-goo eyes at each other, and what looked like an old ID card of some kind. I knew for a fact it was him in the pictures. Partly because he looked a bit like me (with plenty of crazy curls—not bald at all!), but mainly because his name was right there on the ID card: Finn Okenson.

Okenson! That was the name from the newspaper article. Mr Coffee Stain Okenson, the Vampire and Zombie man. It was him! My long-lost dad was a games designer. How cool was that? I guess that explained why Mum had saved the article out of the newspaper. And why he'd seemed so familiar somehow. It all made perfect sense now.

Wow. It was super-weird seeing him in colour, staring back at me. Kind of like those funny mirrors you get at the fair, that make you seem really tall or fat, or all wibbly in the middle. If they did ones that made you look grown-up—that showed you a reflection of yourself in ten years' time—that's what it felt like.

"Hello," I whispered to the mischievous face peering out at me from under a mess of dark curls. He looked like someone who knew *lots* of good jokes. "I'm Noel." Don't ask me why I was talking to a photo—it's not the sort of thing I normally do, honest.

The face in the photo said nothing. Funny that. But then Mum's face appeared, peering round the bedroom door, and I jumped as if I'd been caught doing something really naughty.

"Alright, sleepyhead? You found them then? I dug them out this morning, but you were fast asleep."

I nodded, still feeling too weirded out and excited to manage anything as complicated as words. There he was. My actual flesh-and-blood dad. With my eyes and my hair and half my genes. Did that include the fruit fly ones or not? I never quite worked that one out. And he had the coolest job in the world.

"Will one of them be okay for your family tree do you think?" asked Mum. "Obviously they're a bit out of date now." Her voice was cheery but she looked tired and worried. Perhaps she was nervous in case I didn't like the look of him. In case I didn't want them to try again and be a proper family. "I thought I had a more recent picture actually—a newspaper photo— but I can't find it anywhere I'm afraid."

Oops. "Perfect. Thanks," I managed. And a smile, to show her it was all fine. That I was happy for them. *Noel Okenson*, I thought, trying it out for size. It had a nice ring to it.

"I'm just taking Bauble to school," said Mum. "And then I've got a few errands to run in town. Uncle Mike's downstairs though when you're ready for some breakfast."

Bauble. The anger of the night before had faded away to nothing as I slept. No, not to nothing, actually—it had turned to guilt instead. That's what I could feel sitting in my stomach like a heavy weight when I thought about her. Unless it was hunger…

"Be down in a sec," I called, as Mum disappeared again. "You'll like Bauble," I told the photograph.

Still nothing. Just the same cheeky smile grinning back at me. Of course he'd like her, shared genes or not. He had to.

Bauble had already left when I got downstairs and

it was too late to tell her I was sorry. *Bums*. There were no pancakes waiting for me this time either. Just a pile of cold toast and an Uncle Mike milky tea special.

"Jam, peanut butter, or Marmite?" he asked.

"Chocolate spread please."

Uncle Mike pulled a face. "I thought that was only for special occasions?"

"This *is* a special occasion," I told him. "A special uncle and nephew breakfast."

He grinned. "How can I argue with that? Chocolate spread it is. I won't tell if you don't." He fetched the jar down from the cupboard along with an extra plate. "Think I might join you actually."

It was kind of nice sitting there, just the two of us, chatting about how funny Mr Marsh was, and trying to come up with more biscuit jokes.

"What about Bored-bons?" suggested Uncle Mike, chuckling as he said it. "You know, instead of bourbons?" He wasn't much good at puns, unfortunately. Not like Little Mike, who got paid for writing them. "Or Jabba cakes?" He ran his finger along the top of the chocolate spread jar and licked it. "Mind you, are Jaffa cakes biscuits or cakes? I can never remember."

Bauble would know, I thought. *She knows everything. Apart from why I told her to shut up when she needed me most.* I thought about the promise I'd made Dad in my letter and felt even worse.

"Uncle Mike?" I'd had enough of silly biscuit games all of a sudden. "Have you ever met my real dad?"

"What? Er... no. I haven't." *He* looked worried now, just like Mum. Maybe it was catching. Or perhaps it was because he was lying. I'd heard him giving her new relationship with Finn his blessing the day before, so they *must* have met. I guessed he'd been sworn to silence. "Perhaps you'd be better off talking to your mum," said Uncle Mike.

Huh. Different dad this time, but the same old answer as always.

"More toast?"

I shook my head but he spread me another slice anyway.

"Don't know what was wrong with Bauble this morning," he said, changing the subject. "She didn't tell me a single fascinating fact the whole time I was here. Barely said anything, come to that."

That was it. The weight in my tummy was back again, worse than ever. I wasn't hungry anymore either, which meant it was definitely guilt. And now I had to wait a whole day to tell Bauble how sorry I was. How I didn't mean it.

I spent the rest of the morning watching cartoons, to distract myself from thinking about dads and sisters. It was all too complicated. One minute I'd be planning out exciting adventures with my wild, zombie-zapping new dad, and the next I'd be crunched up with sadness at the thought of what I'd said to Bauble. At the thought of how crushed she must be feeling now she knew the truth about *her* dad. And when Mum got back from doing her jobs and offered to scan in the photos I'd chosen to go on my family tree I told her it didn't matter anymore. That I'd stuck in some drawings of them instead. One more lie to add to all the others.

"How about we get some pizzas in for dinner tonight?" Mum suggested. I thought she was trying to cheer *me* up, but it turned out it was Bauble she was worried about. It seemed like she blamed herself for having handled all the Dad stuff so badly. "I've never seen her so quiet," she said. "Mind, I suppose it's been a funny time for all of us. Maybe a proper family night is exactly what we need."

I didn't say anything. Well, I did say something about pizzas (mainly asking for an extra spicy pepperoni meat feast with cheesy garlic bread and cookie dough ice cream), but I didn't say anything about Bauble. I didn't admit that it was all my fault. Because then I'd have to admit to eavesdropping on the conversation about Mum's new relationship with Finn, as well, and the last thing I wanted to do was mess things up for them. Knowing Mum, she'd be so busy worrying about me—about how I was coping with yet another big emotional shock—that she'd end things before they'd properly begun. No, I had to sort things out with Bauble myself, and as for the rest... well, I'd have to try and be patient. Only a few more months until Christmas...

We walked down to school to pick Bauble up in the afternoon, instead of going in the car. Mum said the fresh air would do us all good. Help us work up an appetite for our pizza party. It worked out pretty well actually, because Mum was still busy chatting to the lollipop lady when Bauble's class came out, so I was able to get my apology in straight away.

"I'm sorry," I said, as soon as I saw her. Her face was set tight in a hard, hurt expression and she refused to look at me. "I didn't mean it," I told her. "About you being jealous. It was a horrible thing to say."

Bauble nodded. "I wasn't jealous," she said. "I was upset about Dad. And I was worried about you. I think you've got it all wrong."

"I know what I heard," I told her.

"Well I know what I saw," she said. "And I'm pretty sure I know who this 'F' is, too. But there's one tiny bit of the puzzle that still doesn't make sense."

"*I* know who it is. It's Finn."

"You're wrong."

I wasn't. I *knew* I wasn't. But I could feel the anger coming back again and I didn't want to fight anymore. "How about we agree to disagree?" I suggested. "Truce?"

"Okay," she said slowly. "I guess so. As long as you promise not to get your hopes up too much…"

"Fine," I said, forcing a smile. "As long as you promise not to mention statistics again."

Bauble's face broke out into a grin. "What's wrong with statistics? Did you know that you're more likely to be killed by a coconut than a shark? And that parents of new babies lose 350 to 400 hours of sleep in the first year?"

What about when you get a new parent? How much sleep do you lose then?

Bauble was on a roll now. "And did you know that over ten percent of the world's salt is used to de-ice roads in America?"

"No, I didn't know that," I admitted, pleased to see she was smiling again. It looked like I was forgiven. "But did you know we're having pizza for dinner tonight? With cheesy garlic bread and cookie dough ice cream?"

"Mmm, that's my favourite fact so far," she said. "I've got another one. Did *you* know we're having a special Family Fun Winter Sports Day to tie in with our 'What Makes Me Me' projects?" She pulled a letter out of her book bag and waved it under my nose. There was a long boring paragraph about the project itself (I didn't bother reading that bit), and then a load of stuff about the actual afternoon and how the games had all been designed to 'celebrate family and friends togetherness and fun'. It sounded pretty good actually.

I skimmed down the list of events with a growing sense of excitement, imagining how amazed everyone would be when I turned up with my award-winning zombie-zapping new dad. When we scooped the medal for the three-legged 'Dads and Lads' race. And then I spotted the date—4th December. Three weeks too early. A whole twenty-one days before Mum and Finn went public with their relationship and I finally, *finally*, got to meet my real dad.

21

TOO MANY SLEEPS 'TIL CHRISTMAS

Do you know what would be really handy here? A montage. I didn't actually know that was the proper word for it but I just asked Bauble and she said that's what it's called. A montage is that bit in a film where they sew lots of little clips together to show time passing by. Like in *Space Runner IV* when it takes Empress Empaline and the snort hogs a whole year to build a new Death Bomber out of broken scraps. No one wants to watch them lasering every single screw into place. So they show you the bit at the beginning, all surrounded by snow, then cut to a spring scene where it's starting to take shape. Then there are a few shots of Empaline sunbathing while the snort hogs finish the exterior, and then more snow through the windows while they give the new control room a final rub down. Everyone knows a whole year's gone by but it's only taken a minute to watch. Barely long enough for Lenny and the Lego Bricks to finish singing the second verse of 'Bob the Battleship Builder' in the background.

I'm not sure what the soundtrack to *my* montage would be. No, wait, I *do* know. Some of Mr Marsh's piano music. That would be perfect. He made a CD for us to listen to in the car, with long rippling runs of notes and short spikey bits that made your ears feel all bright and sparkly inside. Yes, imagine some beautiful piano music playing in the background while you watch us eating our pizza, followed by double helpings of ice cream... while Mum takes us to the seaside for a family fossil-hunt and even more ice cream... while I stare at the Winter Sports Day letter, trying to work out how I can get Finn to go with me... while I secretly track down the address of the Zombies & Vampires computer game company on Laurie's new smartphone (so that Mum can't check my internet search history)... while I write a letter to Finn, asking him to come and do the three-legged Dads and Lads race with me, and reminding him it's nearly my birthday. In fact, there might even be a quick close up of the letter itself...

Dear Mr Okenson (I'm not really sure what to call you. Finn? Dad?)

This is Noel—your son! I hope you don't mind me writing to you like this—I know you and Mum want to keep things secret until after Christmas. She hasn't said anything to me or Bauble (my little sister—I expect Mum's told you all about her) and she doesn't know I'm writing this now.

The thing is, we're having a Family Fun Winter Sports Day on 4th December and I need someone to do the three-legged Dads and Lads race with me. Mum asked the Uncle Mikes but they'll be on holiday (they don't get back until the day after) and I don't want to have to do it with her instead. Or one of the teachers. That would be so lame. It would be AMAZING if you could come! I can't wait to meet you and I bet we'd win! It's at West Elphington Junior School (Longtimber Street) at 1 p.m. The races will be outside on the playing field if it's nice, or in the hall it it's wet (or snowy!).

Please, please, please, please say you'll come. I know you didn't want to be my dad before—I guess babies are hard work—but I'm no trouble at all these days. And nor is Bauble. Don't tell Mum I wrote to you though. She doesn't even know I know and I don't want her to worry or change her mind. But I think it will be a good surprise when she sees you at the sports day. And then it doesn't have to be a secret anymore and we can all be together for Christmas!

I hope to hear from you soon.

Love from Noel xx

P.S. I'm not sure if you know when my birthday is. It's Friday 25th September. Quite soon!

Oh, look, we're at my birthday already. There I am in the montage, waiting by the letterbox for my first ever present from my real dad... and there I am sulking into my birthday pancakes because the postman's been and gone and there's still no parcel from Finn—not even a card...

But don't worry, there I am smiling again, because Mum's made the biggest, chocolatiest birthday cake ever, with my name spelt out in Smarties, and Mr Marsh has popped round with a homemade football birthday card and a giant box of Maltesers. I was so chuffed he remembered that I forgot about Finn for the rest of the night and we all played Twister—the onc game I can beat Bauble at—laughing until it hurt. I *may* have had a bit too much cake and fizzy drink and been slightly sick afterwards, but I'm not putting that in the montage. Or the part where Mr Marsh comes round with Bauble's card and present the next day and we all play Trivial Pursuit and she whoops our asses. You'll just have to imagine that, and all the piano lessons, where I get better and better every week— trust me, I'm getting really good. Oh, and while you're at it perhaps you could imagine the bit where I write *another* letter to Finn in case he didn't get the first one. Perfect. Then I guess we can zoom straight on to Halloween. Or Vampires & Zombies Night, as I'd renamed it in my head...

◆ ◆ ◆

Mum doesn't approve of Trick or Treating so we don't normally dress up for Halloween. But this year was different. This year she'd bought tickets to a special charity Halloween Concert at the Town Hall (Mr Marsh was playing the piano) where you got a free drink at the interval if you went in costume. Bauble seemed to think Mum had chosen to go as a lady vampire to match Mr Marsh's Dracula outfit but I knew better. It was to try and impress Finn, wasn't it? To remind him of his award-winning game. That's why I'd gone for a zombie costume anyway. Perhaps he was dressing up as a zombie too, and then he and Mum could meet up in the middle of the night for a secret Halloween date.

I didn't check the post every single day anymore. But that didn't mean I'd given up hope of hearing from him. On a good day, I told myself he hadn't written back because he wanted it to be a surprise when he turned up at school for our big race. On a bad day, I told myself the work address I'd found for him on the internet wasn't the right one. That he might have moved jobs since then and not got either of the letters I'd sent him. And on a *really* bad day, I worried that he'd read them both and then thrown them in the bin. That even though he was back together with Mum, he still didn't want anything to do with me. There weren't many of those days though, because usually all I had to do was play back the conversation I'd heard outside the kitchen that day—the bit where Mum said '*we don't want to say anything to the kids until we're sure'*—and then I'd feel better again.

Everyone was there at the concert that night—me, Bauble, Mum and the Uncle Mikes. Big Mike was dressed as Frankenstein's monster, with a bolt through his head, while Little Mike had gone as a normal monster, with purple face paint and stick-on yellow warts that kept falling off when he smiled. And I was pretty sure I saw the lady from the optician's talking to the Manzos in the queue. Mrs Manzo was fully dressed this time (thank goodness), and her witch costume was nowhere near as scary as her pork pie and sausage outfit had been.

It was our first ever concert *and* the first time we'd dressed up for Halloween, so Bauble and I were pretty excited. We didn't know what to expect, or even *who* to expect, because the printer had broken and they hadn't been able to make enough programmes for everyone. Between you and me I thought the first half went a bit slowly actually. Partly because I didn't know any of the people playing—apart from Mr Marsh who was accompanying them on the piano—and partly because I started to need the loo. I quite liked the ghost on the trumpet though, with an extra hole cut into his sheet so his lips could reach the mouthpiece, and the zombie who played a jazzed-up version of the James Bond theme on the saxophone. He was pretty cool too. His costume was a bit rubbish compared to the one I imagined Finn wearing, but it was better that mine, and he got a really loud clap at the end. Bauble clapped so hard that one of her stick-on witchy fingernails unstuck itself and flew off over the head of a skeleton pirate lady in the next row.

When I came back from the toilet during the interval, she was wriggling round on her seat like *she* needed to go too. Bauble was doing the wriggling, I mean, not the skeleton pirate lady. But it wasn't because she needed the loo as it turned out, even though she *had* just drunk two free glasses of Fizzy Witches' Brew. It was because she'd sneaked a peek at someone else's programme while I was gone and got all excited when she saw what piece Mr Marsh was going to play.

"Showpan," she kept saying, over and over again, with a big cheesy smile on her face. "*Show*-pan. Of course. Why didn't I think of that before?"

I guessed the Witches' Brew must've done something funny to her super-Bauble-brains because even I could have told her that. Yes. I definitely remembered Mr Marsh saying he'd be doing a Showpan piece at our last lesson. In fact, he even told us the name of it—something like Scaretso Number Two—but Bauble must have been too busy looking at the mountain photograph above his piano to hear. She seemed to spend half of every lesson staring at it over the top of her glasses, like she'd never seen a mountain before. Probably busy trying to calculate the exact height using some complicated maths sum or other.

"Have you seen the greengrocer?" I asked her, changing the subject completely. "He got the end of his loo-roll mummy costume caught in the toilet door and it all started unravelling. Now he's got one mummy leg and one daddy leg!"

It was wasted on Bauble though. She wasn't even listening.

"Where did Mum and the Uncle Mikes go?" I asked.

"What?" She was still grinning away to herself. "Oh, Mum's talking to Mr Marsh, and the Uncle Mikes went to get ice creams from the shop over the road. They promised they'd be back in time for the second half though. In time to hear Mr Marsh do his *Show*-pan." She kept saying it all funny, stretching the *show* bit out extra long so it sounded even more weird than normal. Imagine growing up with a name like Showpan Marsh, I thought.

"What flavour ice cream? I wonder if they do chocchip cookie dough there?"

But Bauble clearly had other things on her mind.

"You know how we agreed not to talk about Mum and the whole kissing Santa in the kitchen thing?" she said. "About who he really was…?"

"My dad, you mean. Finn?" The famous 'F' himself.

She sighed, like she was disappointed in me. Like that was the wrong answer. "You still think it's him, don't you?" she said. "I thought maybe you'd have gone off that idea by now…"

"I don't just *think* it was him," I told her, feeling a familiar stirring of anger inside. "I *know* it was." What I *didn't* know was why she wanted to bring it all up again now, after so many weeks spent avoiding the subject. It had been hard keeping it all to myself— really hard. But I'd done it. Even though I'd been itching to tell her about the letters, about the plan to surprise everyone at the Winter Sports Day with my brand new dad, I hadn't said a word. Because even though I hated not being able to share it with her, I knew it was only for a few months. Not for ever. And I didn't hate it nearly as much as I'd hated fighting with her. So yes, as far as I was concerned the truce was still in place. Even though I was clearly right and she was wrong.

"But what if I was to tell you…"

"Nope," I cut her off before she could say anything else. I knew exactly how this would go otherwise. "We'll only end up falling out."

Bauble sighed again. "Fine. Never mind, here comes Mum anyway. And I guess we'll *all* know soon enough."

Exactly. At least we were both agreed on that.

"Sorry about that," said Mum, as if we'd been lost without her. "I just wanted to wish Mr Marsh luck for his solo. And I promised I'd help tidy up afterwards," she added, pointing to all the chairs and Halloween decorations. "So you two will have to go back with the Uncle Mikes instead. Is that okay?"

"Of course," I said, trying not to smile. Sneaking off to meet my zombie dad, more like.

"No problem," agreed Bauble. She shot me a funny look, and then turned her head towards the door, laughing.

It was Little Mike, holding up a box of vanilla choc-ices like it was the FA cup. Like he'd just scored the winning goal.

The second half seemed to go much quicker than the first. Mr Marsh was brilliant, like I knew he would be. Everyone in the audience stopped fidgeting and coughing and rustling their choc-ice wrappers and listened in total silence.

I imagined it was *me* playing—*my* fingers dancing up and down the keys—while Finn stared in open-mouthed amazement. Like a zombie!

'Wow,' he'd say. *'I never knew I had such a talented son. I couldn't be prouder of you, Noel.'*

And then my mind drifted on to the Winter Sports Day, with the two of us racing down the field, our legs tied together and our arms wrapped tight around each other's waists. The perfect pair. The faster Mr Marsh's fingers went, the faster Finn and I ran, while the rest of the school cheered us on.

'Who's that with Noel?' Mrs Whichey said, remembering my feeble family stick.

'His dad. The famous games designer.'

We crossed the finish line in triumph, just as Mr Marsh finished his piece. And then everyone clapped like we were the most amazing team they'd ever seen, and Mr Marsh got up to take a bow.

"Wasn't he brilliant?" whispered Bauble.

"Totally," I agreed, as Finn and I stepped up to get our winners' rosettes. "The best."

22

ON YOUR MARKS.
GET SET.

I'm not quite sure how I got through the next few weeks. Lots of daydreaming mainly. Lots of telling myself it was all going to be okay. That he'd be there, waiting to surprise me. But, by the time the big day came round, I was so scared and excited I could hardly breathe, let alone force down my breakfast. Which was a shame, because Mum had made a special Winter-Sports-Energy feast to get us ready for an afternoon of chilly races: three pancakes each, filled with mashed bananas and chocolate spread.

"Are you feeling okay?" she asked, looking from my uneaten pancakes to my flushed cheeks. "You seem a bit jittery. You're not nervous about today are you?"

No. Nerves were something you got before a

spelling test you'd forgotten to revise for. Nerves were what you felt before the school play, when you had to sing a line all on your own. Nerves were nothing compared to the squirming, squeezing, fluttering feeling going on in my stomach. To the crazy drumbeat thoughts jumping up and down inside my brain: *What if he's there? What will I say? What if he's not there? What if he didn't get the letter? What if he did get it but he didn't want to see me? What will Mum say when she sees him there?*

"You're not still worrying about the Dads and Lads race are you?" she said.

No. Not worrying. Panicking. Completely freaking out.

"It's a shame the Uncle Mikes couldn't make it," she said, ruffling my hair. "But I've got a funny feeling it's going to be okay."

"What do you mean?" Why was she grinning like a mad woman? Had Finn said something? Did she know? But that meant... *Blistering banana skins!* That meant he was coming! I was actually going to meet my dad! My real-life flesh-and-blood dad!

My stomach stopped fluttering and started flipping. Backwards, forwards, sideways. Faster and faster. This was it! I looked over at Bauble and she was grinning as well. Had she guessed too? Did she realise I'd been right all along?

"Oh, you'll see," said Mum, not wanting to spoil the surprise. "Eat up then. You've got a big day ahead of you."

I bolted down the rest of my pancake, forcing myself to chew. She was right. This was the biggest day of my entire life. The day I finally got to meet my dad!

◆ ◆ ◆

He wasn't there. I'd been camped out in the playground all lunchtime in case he came early, straining my eyes for any tell-tale dark curls peeking out from under a woolly hat—for the face from the newspaper article. I'd memorised everything about him, right down to the freckle by his left eye. There was no sign of him though. Not yet. Other parents came and went, hurrying into the hall out of the cold, but when Mum finally turned up, she was on her own.

The headmaster rang the bell for the end of lunch and I hung back until the last possible moment, willing him to appear at the gates. *Come on, come on. Where are you?*

"You'd better go," said Mum, trying to hurry me inside with the others. "Good luck!"

"Do join us in the hall, Mrs Patermoor," the headmaster called over to her. "The PTA are doing cups of tea and mince pies to warm everyone up before we head out to the field."

"Thank you," said Mum. "I'm waiting for someone actually, but I'll be in as soon as he gets here."

I knew it! He was coming! He was on his way.

"Come on, Noel," she said. "Hurry up, or Mrs Whichey will wonder where you've got to."

"But… but…" I cast one last hopeful look down the road. Where was he?

"Go on. I'll see you out there in a bit." Mum was practically pushing me towards the door.

But… but nothing. I couldn't think of a good enough excuse to stay so I headed off into class, fresh waves of somersaulting insects fluttering round inside my stomach.

I wasn't the only one who was excited. I could hear our class all the way down the corridor. And I could hear Mrs Whichey shouting at Laurie to put Annabelle's apple back in her bag: "It's not an egg, Laurie. And your pencil case isn't a spoon. Sit down now. That means *everybody*. Come on, the sooner you're all sitting quietly and *listening* to me, the sooner you can go out and join the fun. *I said sit down!*"

We were the last class out. No surprise there. The rest of the school was already lined up on the field in their fleecy jogging bottoms and hats and scarves. And wellies. This really wasn't like a normal sports day. The parents were all there too, on the other side of the field, cradling their half-drunk cups of tea and stomping up and down to keep warm. There was Mum! And there, next to her was... no, that wasn't right. It was Mr Marsh. What was he doing there?

I scanned the rest of the row, looking for Finn. He had to be there somewhere. He *had* to. Mum even told the headmaster she was waiting for him...

"Is that him, then?" said Laurie, pointing at Mr Marsh. "The one with your mum?

I hadn't meant to tell him. I hadn't meant to tell anyone. But it came bubbling out of me while Mrs Whichey was going through her endless lists of Winter Sports Day do's and don'ts and I couldn't do anything to stop it. Not even Mrs Whichey could stop it. She moved me to sit with the girls at the back, to stop my 'incessant chatter', but it was too late by then. I'd already blabbed: *'You know how I said my real dad was a famous games designer? I finally get to meet him today… He's coming here to watch the races! To run the three-legged race with me.'*

"No," I told Laurie. "That's my piano teacher. I don't know what he's doing here."

He didn't even have children did he? At least, he never mentioned them.

"Looks like he's coming over," said Laurie. "Maybe he's got a message from your dad… maybe the traffic's really bad and he's running late…"

"I guess." Could that be it? *Please let that be it.*

"Noel!" Mr Marsh beamed. "Just wanted to wish you luck. And report for duty. Your mum said you needed an extra leg for one of the races!"

"What?" I stared stupidly at him, trying to drag my mind back from worrying where Finn was. Trying to make sense of what he was saying. "An extra leg?"

"For the three-legged race," he said. "I was quite the champion three-legged runner in my younger days, you know. Could have gone all the way to the Olympics…"

"But I'm meant to be doing the race with my dad. What's happened? Is he running late?"

Mr Marsh looked surprised. No, more than surprised. He looked shocked. "Your *dad?* Are you sure?"

Of course I was sure. "Mum *said* he was coming. She said…" I played it all back in my head—the conversation at breakfast; what she'd said to the headmaster about waiting for someone—and realised she hadn't *actually* said that at all. Not in so many words. But that's what she meant. It had to be. Otherwise…

Otherwise it meant Mr Marsh was the big surprise. That she'd asked *him* to run the race with me.

The fluttering insects in my stomach were already turning to wasps as I checked my watch. Quarter past one and he still wasn't here. He wasn't coming, was he? He'd never been coming.

I heard the noise before I realised it was me making it. Like a wounded animal, whining in pain.

"Noel?" said Mr Marsh. "What is it? Are you hurt?"

"Leave me alone," I spluttered, between sobs. "You're not my dad."

"Noel. I…"

Not my dad… not my dad… not my dad… The same three words kept whipping round and round inside my head like a tornado. And then everything went strange and swimmy, and someone was holding me up because my legs had stopped working. And then Mum was there, stroking the hair out of my eyes and telling me to calm down. To stop crying.

"Not. My. Dad."

"Shh, Noel. It's alright. Come on. I've got you. That's it. Look at me."

I opened my eyes and stared around in confusion. The field had gone. I was standing outside the Year 4 classroom next to Mum, with cold, wet cheeks and a raw ache in my throat.

"He's not coming, is he?" I croaked. "My dad. Finn."

Mum's face was pale and pinched-looking. "No, sweetheart. I told you, I haven't heard from him in years."

"I just thought… when you said about the Dads and Lads race…" *I thought you were together. I thought we were going to be a family.* How could I have been so stupid? Whoever it was she'd been talking about in the kitchen that day, it wasn't him.

Maybe I'd imagined the whole thing.

"Oh, Noel, I'm sorry. I thought you'd be pleased I'd found someone to do the race with you."

Who cared about the race? I thought my dad was coming back for me. I thought we had a future together. But it was just me and my stupid imagination again.

"I thought you *liked* Mr Marsh." Mum clutched at her chest as if someone had punched her. Like the mere thought of Finn was a physical blow to her heart.

"I *do* like him," I said, trying to get my feelings back under control. It wasn't his fault, after all. Not that he'd like *me* anymore. Not after he'd given up his afternoon to help me do a race and I'd screamed in his face like a tantrumy two-year old. "I don't know what came over me…"

I guess I should have told her about the letters. Tried to explain. But I didn't. I let her wrap me up in her arms and hug me tight, hugging her back as if my life depended on it. I might not have a dad who cared but at least I had a mum who loved me. I squeezed my arms tight around her waist and cried into her winter jacket, waiting for the hurt to stop.

23

Go!

Mum texted Mr Marsh when I was feeling better and he came to find us, with Bauble in tow.

"Someone here was a bit worried about you," he said, laying a gloved hand on my shoulder. "We both were."

"I'm really sorry," I murmured, cheeks burning in the cold morning air. "I don't know what happened..."

"Don't worry about it," said Mr Marsh, kindly. "You've obviously had a lot of things going on lately. Lots to get your head round."

I nodded. Not that I *had* got my head round any of it. My head had been off somewhere else entirely, doing crazy circles all on its own.

Mr Marsh was being so nice about it all. "It can get a bit much sometimes, can't it? Happens to the best of us. Just as long as you're okay, that's all that matters."

I nodded again. Bauble reached out and squeezed my hand but she didn't say anything. No *I told you so*.

"And don't worry about the race," said Mr Marsh. "I quite understand. I'd like to stay and watch though, if that's alright?"

"I'd rather you ran it with me," I told him, still feeling guilty for shouting at him like that. For losing it. "Seeing as you're practically an Olympic gold champion," I added, trying to make a joke out of it all. "That's if you still want to."

"It would be my honour," he said. "How about a quick practice on the way back?" He linked his arm round my waist and stuck out his left leg. "Come on!"

I stuck out my right leg next to his, as if they were tied together with an invisible rope, and off we went, half-running, half-stumbling, all the way back to the field, with Mum and Bauble giggling behind us. Even I was laughing by the end, despite my disappointment. Despite everything. It *was* pretty funny.

No one said anything when I rejoined my class, which was a relief. Mrs Whichey must have had a quiet word with them while I was gone. *Don't say anything to Noel about him doing a complete nutso in front of everyone.* Laurie gave me a friendly nudge in the ribs and slipped me a furry-looking jelly baby out of his pocket, but apart from that no one paid me any attention at all. They were too busy watching the start of the Year Three Christmas Stocking race—exactly like a sack race, only the sacks had been painted red and green to look more festive—cheering for their little brothers and sisters. Or just cheering randomly. Bauble should have been there racing with the rest of her class too but they were already at the halfway mark by the time she reached the start line.

"Don't worry about getting in it," Miss Kershaw shouted, handing the last sack to Bauble. "Just run!"

So that's what she did. She held the sack up over her head like a Christmas hat and tore off up the field after the others. And, because she didn't have to worry about tripping over her own wellies all the time, she even managed to catch them up. You should've seen the look on her face as she overtook Chloe Corston!

"Hey, that's not fair," yelled Chloe, stumbling into second place after Bauble. "She cheated!"

But the headmaster didn't miss a beat. "Well, ladies and gentlemen," he said, booming into his microphone as the winter sun bounced off his shiny bald head. "It seems we've got ourselves *two* winners in the renamed Stocking and Elf Hat race. Let's have a big hand for Holly Patermoor and Chloe Corston!"

The crowd went wild. Well, me, Mum and Mr Marsh did. I could hear them whooping and cheering all the way across the field when Bauble got her red rosette. She'd never won a single sports event in her entire life so it was a pretty big deal—even if it was only for fun. And totally against the rules. Mind you, that wasn't the only bit of rule-bending that went on that morning. Wait until you hear what happened in the famous three-legged Dads and Lads race…

I'd be lying if I said I wasn't still looking out for Finn during the other races. I even had a bit of a check while I was waiting for my turn in the Round Robin Relay. You know, just in case he really was running late. But I managed to keep it together without having another meltdown in front of the entire school, which was a bonus. I kept telling myself that even though he and Mum weren't a couple after all, that didn't mean *I* couldn't still get to know him. It didn't mean they'd *never* get back together again. And even if he didn't come to the race, all that meant was my letters must have got lost in the post. Or maybe it was his letters back to me that got lost—the ones that said he was dying to meet me but had an important meeting at the exact same time as the Winter Sports Day. It's amazing what you can make yourself believe when you put your mind to it. When you really want something to be true. When you *need* it to be.

That's not to say I wasn't excited when the headmaster told all the Year 5 and 6 boys to take their places for the Dads and Lads three-legged race. Even if Finn *was* a no-show. It was nice of Mr Marsh to come and do it with me, and now I'd got over my little episode I was determined to enjoy it. He'd already collected a Velcro leg tie from one of the teachers and was doing exaggerated warm-up exercises to make everyone laugh. He might not have been a proper relation—not like all the other dads lining up to take their places—but I was still glad he was on my team. He always managed to make me smile. We strapped our legs together, found a space at the end of the group and waited for the start whistle.

On your marks, get set...

"STOP!" came a loud cry from behind. "Wait for us!"

Finn? I thought, whipping round to see. Only I'd forgotten I was still tied to Mr Marsh and I lost my balance, landing flat on my face with a loud tear of Velcro.

"Woah, steady on," Mr Marsh said, bending down to help me. "The race hasn't even started yet. And I hate to tell you this, Noel, but you're going the wrong way. That's *exactly* where I went wrong in the Olympics." He glanced over my shoulder and laughed. "I hope your teacher's got some more leg ties because it looks like the cavalry's arrived."

I pulled myself up and turned to see. It wasn't Finn. It was the Uncle Mikes, charging up the field in their holiday shorts and t-shirts. And, in Big Mike's case, flip-flops.

"Please don't start without us," panted Little Mike. "We took a taxi all the way from the airport to get here on time."

The headmaster stood staring—the start whistle hanging uselessly off his bottom lip—as my two crazy uncles ran and flip-flopped the last few metres to reach us. I knew exactly how he felt.

"But… but… I thought you were still on holiday?" I stammered, trying to take it all in.

"We were," said a tanned-looking Big Mike. "But we managed to get an earlier flight. We didn't want you to miss out on your big race." That's when he spotted Mr Marsh. "Though it looks like you had it all covered anyway. Hello again," he said, giving Mr Marsh a cheery slap on the shoulder. "Good to see you. Room for two more on the team?"

Mr Marsh grinned. "Absolutely. Might need a couple of extra leg ties though."

"Coming right up," said Little Mike.

It was bonkers. Brilliantly bonkers. Before long, we were all strapped together in a long line—the world's first ever five-legged team in a three-legged Dads and Lads race. Everyone around us—all the other boys and men—were laughing out loud. They even shuffled over to give us the best space on the starting line.

"That is *so* cool," said the skinny new boy in Year 5. "I wish I had as many dads as you!"

I opened my mouth to explain—*none of them are actually my real dad*—and then shut it again. Because it didn't matter. At that exact moment in time, I wouldn't have swapped them for anything. For anyone.

We didn't win. Surprisingly enough. We didn't even come close. But I felt like a winner all the same. Every time one of us stumbled—usually Big Mike, tripping over his own flip-flops—we all fell over together in a tangled, giggling heap. And everyone watching cheered when we got back up again. I could hear Mum squawking like an overexcited parrot as she ran along the edge of the course with her camera, yelling, "Go Team Patermoor! You can do it!" I would have waved at her only I didn't have any hands. I just grinned instead. I couldn't *stop* grinning. Especially when we tumbled over the finish line to the biggest, loudest cheer of the whole afternoon. And later, when I finally remembered about Finn—much later—I was almost glad he hadn't turned up.

Almost.

24

F IS FOR FOOL

One more time, I told myself. One last try at getting hold of my real dad. And if I *still* didn't hear back from him, then… well, I didn't know the answer to that one. I wasn't planning on finding out either. He really would write back this time. Or ring. Or turn up on the doorstep, asking to start again. He had to.

I wrote it that night, once the magic of our five-legged race had finally worn off. I'd felt like a hero all afternoon, with people I hardly knew coming up to tell me how much my team had made them laugh. How they wanted to copy me at the next sports day. Even Mrs Whichey said how funny it was. She said she'd never forget the sight of Big Mike's blue toes and goose-bumped legs as he belly-flopped over the line, gasping out his own special version of 'We are the

Champions' by Queen.

We must have relived it a hundred times at home afterwards too, over hot snotlates and pus-turd creams, giggling at the photos Mum had taken while she was running along beside us. But the sadness hit me all over again when I was on my own, getting ready for bed. I'd been so sure he'd come. That Mum would see us together and realise they didn't need to keep their relationship secret any longer. Only it turned out there wasn't a relationship *to* keep secret. Not with Finn anyway. So who was 'F' then? *Was* she seeing someone or wasn't she? I'd got myself in such a muddle over everything I couldn't tell which bits were real anymore, and which bits were all in my head.

Maybe it wasn't too late though. Maybe it was just a case of getting her and Finn together again, so they'd remember how they felt about each other.

Dear Finn (Dad),

It's me again—Noel. I'm not sure whether you got my other letters about the Winter Sports Day. If not, it doesn't matter because you've missed it now. But I do still want to meet you. I still want you to be my dad.

Perhaps you could come to our house for

Christmas? (The address is at the top of this letter. I've put our phone number in too in case you want to ring first. But maybe you could pretend to be my friend Laurie if Mum answers. Just so we don't spoil the surprise). Mum always says we should look out for people who are on their own at that time of year so I'm sure it will be fine. And the Uncle Mikes always buy a really big turkey so there'll be plenty of food to go round. Please say you'll come. It would be the best Christmas present ever to finally meet you.

Hope to see you in a few weeks,
Lots of love,
Noel xxx

I felt better for having written it; for having something fresh to hope for. It didn't make getting to sleep any easier though—there were still too many thoughts chasing round my brain for that, but on the upside that meant I was still awake when Mum went to bed. Which meant I could sneak back down to her study for another stamp and envelope without having to answer any tricky questions. I sealed it all up and wrote our address on the back (if undelivered, please return), so at least then I'd know if it had got there.

Shame I hadn't thought of that the last two times. And then I added an extra message along the bottom of the envelope to be on the even more safe side: *Please write back and let me know if you're coming or not. Even if you don't want to be my dad I'd rather you told me.*

I did fall asleep eventually, with the letter tucked under my pillow for safe-keeping, while I dreamt about running a relay race with Mum and the headmaster. An Olympic relay race. Only instead of a baton we all had to pass a flip-flop to each other and everyone started booing when I dropped it. Still, at least it made a change from dreaming about dads. And, when I woke up in the morning, I got straight into my clothes, did a passing wish under every single one of the wishing bows in my doorway, and slipped outside to the postbox.

"Good luck," I told the envelope as it disappeared inside. No going back now.

◆ ◆ ◆

"What were you doing outside earlier?" whispered Bauble at breakfast. She wasn't actually eating any breakfast because her spoon was sitting in a glass of water while she read about something called 'light refraction' on her tablet. "I saw you out the window."

"Sending a letter to my dad," I whispered back. I guessed the truce really was over now—now we knew that 'F' wasn't Finn after all. "Asking him to come for Christmas. Don't tell Mum though. I want it to be a surprise." I didn't want her to say 'no', which was almost the same thing.

Bauble's eyes narrowed. "What did you do that for?" she hissed. Mum was upstairs collecting dirty washing but she'd be back at any moment. "You'll ruin everything."

"Huh?"

"This will be their first Christmas together," said Bauble, putting down her tablet to focus on her glaring. "It's going to be a bit awkward with your dad there too, isn't it?"

"*Whose* first Christmas together?"

"Mummy and Mr Marsh… and Fred."

What? I almost spat out my Dino Rocks. Mum and Mr Marsh? No way.

"Don't be silly," I said. "He's our piano teacher. And who's this Fred guy, anyway? How many secret boyfriends has she got?" The name rang a bell though. Fred... Fred... Yes, of course! That's what Big Mike called Mr Marsh that time they both came round for lunch.

Bauble let out a long sigh. Like she couldn't believe she had such a doofus duh-brain for a brother. "That's his name—Fred Marsh. Short for Frédéric."

I really did spit out my Dino Rocks that time, sending half-chewed flecks flying onto Bauble's screen. *Schwoom! Splat! Take that, 'Let's Learn about Light Refraction'!* She almost had me going there for a minute.

"His name's Showpan," I told her. *Now* who was the doofus? She must have caught the Fred disease from Uncle Mike. "I can't believe you've forgotten that already."

"His name's Fred," she insisted. "As in Frédéric Chopin—spelt C-H-O-P-I-N. *That's* what was confusing me. I'd been looking up the wrong name, because I thought it began with an 'S'. Everything else made sense: the photograph above his piano (I was *sure* it was one of Mummy's)... the little cartoon pictures he did in our notebooks, just like the robin you saw on the postcard... the story about losing an imaginary bracelet… but it wasn't until I saw his name in the programme that I finally realised what an idiot I'd been. There it was in black and white: Fred Marsh, playing Scherzo No. 2 by Frédéric Chopin."

Woah.

Double woah.

Blistering Banana Skins times one hundred.

I guess I knew instinctively she was right. It all made perfect sense. But that didn't mean I wanted to believe it. Because if it really was true—if Mum and Mr Marsh really were a proper couple (I didn't even want to *think* about the two of them kissing)—where did that leave Finn? How were they ever going to get back together again now?

"Alright then, Miss Clever Clogs," I said, as if it was all Bauble's fault. "How come they haven't said anything to us then?"

She shrugged. "I guess they wanted to see how things went for a bit. I don't know. *You're* the one who said they were waiting until Christmas."

"But…" But that was when I thought it was Finn. "And what about the Father Christmas outfit? Explain that. Why would Mr Marsh be parading round our kitchen in swimming trunks and a Santa hat if they were trying to keep things quiet? Why would *anyone* be wearing swimming trunks and a Santa hat?"

Bauble shrugged again. "I'm still working on that one. Perhaps we should just be happy for them though? I mean, he makes Mummy happy and that's a good thing, isn't it?"

Was it? I didn't know what it was really, apart from a shock. It was definitely one of those. The last in a long line of shocks.

"We are the champions, my friend," sang Mum, waltzing in through the kitchen door with a basket of dirty clothes. "And we'll keep on washing 'til the end."

Hmm. Mum *did* seem pretty happy these days. Especially now all the Dad stuff was out in the open.

She planted kisses on our heads as she danced past.

"Before I forget," she said, "Mr Marsh has invited us all round for dinner tonight, to celebrate Bauble's sporting victory. And the triumphant non-victory of the five-legged team, of course. Spaghetti Bolognese, with crumble and ice cream for pudding. The Uncle Mikes are coming too."

"That sounds lovely," said Bauble pulling a *see-I-told-you-so* face behind Mum's back. "I can't wait."

"Oh, and he wondered if you wanted to watch the

football highlights with him afterwards, Noel. Something to do with that player you like—what's his name again?"

"Petro Ollander."

"That's the one," said Mum. "First match since his injury—is that right?"

I nodded. Yes, that was right. And Bauble was right too. It *did* sound lovely. But what if she was right about *everything?* What if I really had ruined things by inviting Mum's old boyfriend to Christmas dinner?

"Should I tell her?" I whispered.

Bauble went for a third shrug. Not exactly the most helpful answer ever.

"Tell me what?" said Mum, spinning back round for another sneaky kiss on the forehead.

"Er… that I'm going to tidy the tissues and football magazines out from under my bed? And do the hoovering."

Wait a minute. Hoovering? Where did that come from? It must have been the guilt talking. Guilt, panic, and another triple helping of confusion. Every time I thought I'd got all the dad stuff straight in my head, something else happened to swirl it all up again. Another dad whirlpool whizzing round in my brain.

"My goodness," said Mum, pretending to collapse backwards in surprise. "What have I done to deserve this? It's like Christmas come early!"

25

LETTER SNOW, LETTER SNOW, LETTER SNOW!

The letter arrived a week later, addressed to Mr N Patermoor, with the computer game company's return address printed on the back of the envelope. Just when I'd finally managed to convince myself it didn't matter that I'd written to Finn again. That he was never going to reply anyway. That there was no way in a million years he'd be waiting on our doorstep on Christmas Day.

"Is that the post?" said Mum, sticking her head out the kitchen door.

"No." I hid the envelope behind my back, wondering when the lies were ever going to stop. *What had I done?* I'd thought about it all so much in the last few days and realised Bauble was right. As usual. I just wanted Mum to be happy too. And she and Finn would never have worked out. She'd always be worrying in case he ran away again. *I'd* always be worrying in case he ran away again.

"Are you sure about that?" said Mum, pointing to the mini-mountain of junk mail and Christmas cards by my feet.

"Oh. Er, yes. *That's* the post, but... but..." The excuse died on my lips. I couldn't do it anymore. "I'm really sorry, Mum. I think I might have done something silly."

"You haven't trodden on a present again have you?" She must have been thinking about the new Einstein glasses case she'd ordered for Bauble's birthday. The Einstein glasses case I accidentally squashed under my school shoe in my hurry to see if Finn had sent me a card. It was all a bit awkward at the time, which is why it didn't make it into my montage.

"No," I said, lifting up my feet to check. "I don't think so. But I might have accidentally... well, no, not accidentally... I might have sort of asked my real dad to come for Christmas. And I didn't think he actually would, only..." I pulled the letter out from behind my back. "Only this just came. I'm sorry. I'm really, really sorry…"

"Hey," said Mum, almost skidding on the post mountain in her hurry to reach me. Perhaps she thought I was about to unleash Winter Sports Day Meltdown II: the enhanced special effects sequel. "It's okay, Noel. It doesn't matter. Whatever it is I'm sure we can sort it out."

She took me into the sitting room and sat me down on the sofa. "Now, why don't you start again? Right from the beginning."

The beginning? The *very* beginning? Really?

But that's exactly what I did. I told her everything, pouring out the whole sorry mess from Bauble's first sighting under the wishing bow to the last letter I'd sent. I even told her how Bauble had worked it all out. About her and Mr Marsh.

It was scary, finally admitting to it all, but it felt good too. It felt like a massive weight had been lifted off my shoulders, even though I hadn't known it was there.

"I'm sorry," I said again.

"No," said Mum, squeezing my hand. "*I'm* the one who should be sorry. You shouldn't *have* to go skulking round behind my back looking for answers."

She squeezed tighter, almost crushing my fingers. "I thought I was protecting you but it seems like I've made everything ten times worse. Of *course* you want to meet your real dad. That's only natural."

Did I still want to meet him?

"I should have been honest from the start, only… only I didn't want you to get hurt. I didn't know how to explain why he didn't want to be with us. And all these years, he never once tried to get in contact… never once asked to see you…" She let go of my throbbing fingers and pointed to the letter. "But I guess I underestimated him. Which is great. I'm glad." She didn't *look* that glad. Her mouth was smiling but the rest of her face wasn't. "Would you like some space to read it in private? Or we can look at it together if you'd rather."

Yes. No. I don't know. I couldn't even bring myself to open it. I wished I'd never written to him in the first place. And yet… he *was* my dad.

"Can you do it?"

Mum nodded, easing the envelope out of my clenched fingers. She tore it open along the top and pulled out a folded sheet of A4 paper. A typed letter.

"Oh," she said, the fake smile slipping away again.

"Oh dear."

"What is it? What does it say?"

"It's from one of the secretaries at the games company. She says Finn hasn't worked there for a few years now. She's forwarded on your letter to the home address they had on the system but it's quite possible that's out of date too." Mum let out a long sigh. "She says she's very sorry she couldn't be more helpful because it sounded like it was important from what you'd written on the back of the envelope. And she says she didn't even know Mr Okenson *had* any children, but she wishes you the best of luck."

"I see." I didn't know what to say to that. I didn't know what to feel.

"I'm sorry, Noel," said Mum. "But even if he didn't get your letter, we'll find another way of tracking him down."

"That's okay. I'm not sure I want to see him anymore." As I was saying it I realised it was true. Would Winter Sports Day have been any better if Finn had actually turned up? How could it? We had the most fun out of anyone there. And did it matter that my family tree looked different to everyone else's? With red sausages instead of extra relatives? Not really. I got to live next door to the two best uncles in the whole wide world. Uncles who'd give up the end of their holiday just to run down a freezing field with me. And I had the brainiest, Baubliest little sister in the universe, the loveliest mum, and the funniest piano teacher and Petro Ollander fan anyone could hope for. My family might be a different shape to everyone else's but it was still full of love and laughter.

"And if you're not comfortable with me seeing Fred, that's fine too," said Mum. "We can go back to being friends. You and Bauble are my top priority and you always will be…"

"No," I interrupted her. "It still seems a bit funny, but good funny. Just like him."

I could see the relief in her eyes. I could see how much he meant to her.

"And I think Dad would have liked him too," I said. "Not Finn—Nick, my *real* dad."

It wasn't until much later—long after the hugging and the promises to be honest with each other from now on were over—that I realised she still hadn't explained about the swimming trunks and Santa hat. Perhaps it was best not to know…

26

UNDERNEATH
THE WISHING BOW

There weren't any more letters. Maybe Finn had moved house again like the secretary said and he never got my last one either. Or maybe he had got it but wasn't interested. It hardly seemed to matter anymore. We were all having too much fun, decorating the house for Christmas with homemade paperchains, learning carols on the piano with Fred, helping the Uncle Mikes make the biggest, most marzipan and icingy cake ever, playing Elf Chase on our tablets (well, I was—Bauble was doing some super-brainy quiz thing on hers) and working on a new biscuit and food-related joke book while Mum was upstairs wrapping presents.

I had a last-minute attack of nerves on Christmas Eve as we were putting out the sherry and mince pie for Santa but it didn't last long. He wasn't going to come, was he? Finn, I mean, not Father Christmas. And I was right. He didn't. It was just the six of us—me, Bauble and Mum, Mike, Mike and Fred. The perfect number. The perfect day.

"Oh, I almost forgot," said Mum as we tidied away the torn wrapping paper. "I've got two more presents upstairs." My ears pricked up at that—*more* presents?—but they weren't for us as it turned out. Which I was pretty glad about once I saw what they were…

"Wow, thank you," said Little Mike, staring at the calendar with a mix of horror and amusement. "It's er… just what we always wanted!"

"Oh my goodness," said Fred, when Mum gave him his copy. "I'd almost forgotten about this."

There it was, the West Elphington Charity Calendar, starring twelve local shopkeepers and businesspeople, in all their swimming-costumed glory. All photographed by Mum. There was Mrs Manzo, with her pork pie hat and sausage necklace. And there was Mr March, who turned out to be the greengrocer, in his green swimming trunks and matching grape wig. March wasn't his name after all then, just the month underneath his picture. In the same way that the lollipop lady's June—with her bikini balancing cream cakes—was really Moira, one of Mum's friends who worked in the baker's.

"Obviously they saved the best 'til last," said Mum, with a wink.

"No, I can't bear to see," laughed Fred, hiding his face behind an escaped bit of wrapping paper as Uncle Mike flipped over onto December.

You've guessed it. The picture for December was Fred himself, wearing a pair of red swimming trunks and a Santa hat (the very same Santa hat he was wearing now, in fact), with a bit of silver and red tinsel strung round his neck. Yes, there he was in the corner of *our* sitting room, pretending to play *our* piano, smiling over his shoulder at the camera. At Mum. He looked ridiculously happy, like his Christmas had come early that year.

◆ ◆ ◆

I saw them that night when I went back downstairs to get the football book Fred had given me. He still hadn't taken his Santa hat off and it caught on the wishing bow as he leaned in to kiss Mum. It was every bit as yuck as I'd expected. But kind of nice too, so long as I didn't have to watch. I turned round and looked at Bauble instead, who'd appeared beside me on the stairs as if by magic. I looked at her bright blue eyes shining behind her bright bogey glasses. At the massive grin stretched across her face.

"Happy Christmas," she whispered. It almost sounded like a question. *Happy Christmas?*

"Best one ever," I whispered back.

The End